friends to the end

Other titles in the Summit High series:

friends to the end

Matt Tullos
with Tracey L. Bumpus

BROADMAN
& HOLMAN
PUBLISHERS

Nashville, Tennessee

0-8054-1977-2

Published by Broadman & Holman Publishers, Nashville, Tennessee
Page Design: Anderson Thomas Design, Nashville, Tennessee
Typesetting: PerfecType, Nashville, Tennessee
Editorial Team: Vicki Crumpton, Janis Whipple, Kim Overcash

Dewey Decimal Classification: F
Subject Heading: HIGH SCHOOLS—FICTION
Library of Congress Card Catalog Number: 99-37831

Library of Congress Cataloging-in-Publication Data
Tullos, Matt, 1963–
    Friends to the end / Matt Tullos.
      p.   cm. — (Summit High series ; bk. 6)
    Summary: Friends at Summit High struggle with issues involving teen pregnancy,
drug use, and a bombing incident while some among them turn to their Christian
faith for strength.
    ISBN 0-8054-1977-2 (pbk.)
    [1. Friendship Fiction. 2. Christian life Fiction. 3. High schools Fiction.
4. Schools Fiction.] I. Title. II. Series: Tullos, Matt, 1963– Summit High series ; 6.
PZ7.T82316Fr   1999
[Fic]—dc21

99-37831
CIP

1 2 3 4 5 03 02 01 00 99

Dedication

To Caleb

Prologue

Everyone expected "See You at the Pole" to be different this year, but no one expected to see a crowd of such magnitude. One of the local network affiliates chose to broadcast its early morning show across the street from the massive gathering of students.

"Many speculate that this event at Summit High School is one of the biggest risks Indianapolis has ever taken," one reporter began. "Over a dozen threats have been made by a secret group whose members call themselves 'The Association.' They've stated in no uncertain terms that if this prayer event is allowed, a church in the Indianapolis area would be destroyed. Perhaps by fire, perhaps by a bomb. The police have taken these threats very seriously and have requested that all churches close their doors today. A historic school board meeting Monday shocked everyone. As you've probably heard, the school board planned to prohibit this gathering, but pastors from almost every denomination stood in support of the students. Now, they can only pray. And pray they will."

Across town, The Association's plan had been executed flawlessly. They placed the bomb in the small church in less than two minutes and left quickly to go into hiding and celebrate their accomplishment. But they had underestimated the efforts of a former member named A. C.

Time became A. C.'s greatest enemy as he tried to decide what to do. His mind transported him back to all the television coverage from Columbine High. Scenes flashed before his mind's eye. The shock of the nation, the hatred of every parent and teacher toward the shooters. For the first time in his life, it seemed, he really cared about someone else. And he knew he had to get to the bomb in St. Luke's.

He flew through traffic, his heart bouncing furiously off his rib cage. He knew the schedule. He had ten minutes. As he turned into the church parking lot, he looked for any sign that people might be inside. It looked empty so far. As he got out of his car he looked down the avenue and saw Elliot's Camaro fleeing the scene and wondered if he'd been seen. Probably not—otherwise, they would've turned around. Chances are The Association would have executed A. C. if they caught him. Life was as cheap as garbage to Elliot, just as it used to be to A. C. But in the span of twenty-four hours, A. C. had become The Association's worst enemy.

A. C. knew that the back entrance was the plan in every scenario they had created. He quickly, silently, raced to the back entrance of the church and saw the scraps of a plastic bag and small strands of wire that Elliot had carelessly discarded. A. C.

reached for the doorknob. Locked. Elliot had had the presence of mind to lock the door! A. C. backed up and kicked the door, praying that the bomb sat further inside the building.

He cracked the face of the door but it didn't open. Once again, with even more anger and force, he kicked the door. This time it opened. The sudden high-pitched sound of the security system greeted A. C., adding greater stress. At that moment he realized that the church's security system must have been engaged when Elliot and company placed the bomb. This left him with even less time to do his work. The police would be on their way.

It was 7:27 A.M. He knew three minutes stood between him and a terrible explosion. He ran through the dark corridors of the small building, feeling his way through, tripping on the tables and chairs in the old neighborhood church.

Finally, just ahead, he saw the familiar blinking red light. During their planning, Elliot and A. C. had often set the timer and imagined the detonation and chaos that would follow. Now A. C. walked cautiously toward the bomb and peered into the LED clock. Two minutes. Just as planned.

With trembling hands, he searched the walls for a light switch. He turned the light on and pulled the wire cutters out of the front pocket of his jeans. From his back pocket he grabbed the handwritten diagram Elliot had given him the week before.

"God, if you're out there, don't let this thing go off," A. C. whispered under his breath. "Red, they're dead. Blues, you lose," he chanted three times, trying to relax. It was the reminder Elliot had given A. C. when A. C. was to help in planting the bomb.

A. C. slowly moved the crude wire cutters closer to the blue wire. Forty-five seconds and counting. Slowly, he applied pressure to the handle of the wire cutters and cut the wire. The clock stopped, and a split second later the LED screen went blank.

A. C. ran for the door and tripped on a chair in the hall. His fall jammed his head into the corner of the doorframe. Dizzy, yet determined to flee, A. C. stumbled out the door and into the morning sunlight. He heard the approaching sirens and raced into the protection of nearby bushes.

A. C. nervously watched the scene unfold at St. Luke's Christian Church. He saw the bomb squad vehicle arrive, followed by three other patrol cars. A. C. knew he had risked his own freedom by reporting the bomb.

Three officers wearing protective armor walked cautiously to the open door. After a short discussion they went inside. One of the officers yelled out to the others, "It's real! Clear the area!"

A. C.'s heart raced as he watched from his hiding place. He felt certain the bomb had been diffused, but that didn't stop him from worrying about the safety of the officers.

This was certainly a change for him. Little more than a month ago, he had no respect for authority. He hated school. He hated his life. He wanted everyone around him to experience the full wrath of his existence. "Better to burn out than to fade away," he'd often said. He never looked to the future. He never pictured himself having kids or a thirty-year mortgage. He would never live that long, he had thought. So his new attitude confused him.

Two officers began to talk heatedly. A. C. was curious about what was going on. He looked in all directions, and then slowly, carefully moved over to a row of hedges that bordered a house across the street. Adrenaline still pulsed through his body, giving him a rush.

He strained to hear what the officers were saying over the drone of traffic and police radios. As he listened, he was unaware of what was happening just behind him.

"Freeze!" an officer shouted sternly.

A. C. could do nothing *but* freeze. "Put your hands behind your head and turn around slowly."

A. C. had been through this drill before. In the past, it had only annoyed him. But those were the days when the police busted him for minor incidents. This could be serious.

"What's your problem?" A. C. asked.

"Shut up!" the officer demanded.

A. C. turned around and saw a tall, thin, middle-aged, plain-clothes officer. Two others hurried over to provide back-up.

"What's going on?" A. C. asked.

"We know who you are. Personally, I didn't think you'd be dumb enough to show your face around here."

A. C. searched for his usual sarcastic wit, but before he could say anything, the officer continued, "So why don't you save both of us a lot of time and tell me exactly what you did here."

"What *I* did?" A. C. asked angrily.

"Don't play dumb, A. C. And don't lie to us. We know more than you think. Just tell us the truth. Where did you get the stuff to make the bomb? And what's this group all about?"

"Group?" A. C. shot back.

"Don't play games with us," the detective said sternly.

A. C. paused, as he tried to make a choice about how to explain his presence. From the sound of it, he wouldn't be able to satisfy them with any explanation. "I want a lawyer," he said in resignation.

"I bet you do," another officer spoke up rudely.

"Shut up, Ted," the detective said, still holding the gun on A. C.

"I'm clean. Can I please put my hands down?" A. C. said angrily.

The plain-clothed detective looked over to one of the uniformed officers. "Search and cuff him, Jim. Send him over to the station right now. Channel 7 is already here. If they see this, it'll be a circus out here."

The officer grabbed A. C.'s arms and yanked them behind him. He felt the muscles in his shoulders strain as the cuffs were closed.

His head throbbed as he sat in the back of the patrol car. "Aren't you going to read me my rights?" A. C. asked the officer.

"Me? Nah. Don't plan to ask you any questions. I'm just the deliveryman on this one. Of course, if you want to talk, go ahead," the officer said.

"I didn't do anything," A. C. said louder.

"Really?" the officer said with a smile as he glanced in the rearview mirror. "Well, I am so glad to hear you say that, son.

Join the 'not-guilty club.' Being in the back seat like that seems to make kids like you innocent. Happens every time. Strange."

"I'm the one who tipped you off. I don't guess it would hurt my case to tell you that."

"OK."

"Is that all you have to say?" A. C. replied angrily.

"That's all I have to say. I'm not interested in small talk."

A. C. sank into despair. Wouldn't you know the one time he did something truly heroic, he would be falsely charged?

The police read his rights, booked A. C., notified his grandmother, and then transferred him to the juvenile detention center. The officers refused to let him talk to anyone. The investigators didn't even come by to question him. He was led into the high-security area of the center, where the guard locked the cell door and left without a word.

When A. C. realized no one would be interviewing him, he slammed his fist on the wall and screamed in frustration. The familiar feelings of loneliness and despair invaded him. He sat in silence, trembling. He could hear the muffled sound of a television newscast: "The Metro police chief announced today that the department is on the verge of uncovering the source behind the bomb threats that have plagued the Metro school district and local churches for the past six weeks. Although no names were released, a suspect has been apprehended."

Kandi Roper and Justin Henderson were relieved as they drove to the Good Times Grill. A tremendous weight was lifted from their shoulders after "See You at the Pole." They thought about the reports that could have hit the news, reports of violence and bombs. Thank God, though, the reports never came. The prayer around the flagpole had brought TV news crews from as far away as Muncie, which gave the event even more notoriety. But more importantly, the students at Summit were now unified. People they had never dreamed would participate had come that morning to pray.

"Is this weird?" Kandi asked, smiling.

"What? This? Us?" Justin asked in a curious tone.

"A few weeks ago I thought our friendship was history."

"Really?" Justin said, again sounding surprised. "Kandi, I told you we'd be friends, didn't I?"

"And you meant it?" Kandi asked.

"Well," Justin said, and then paused, letting out a long sigh. "I guess I wanted to mean it, but it's hard to maintain a friendship with a girl when you're wildly jealous—insanely jealous—of the guy she's dating."

"Nerd," Kandi said playfully.

"No, really, it's true. I wanted to be friends, and I still want to be friends; but I was going through this, this thing, about you that just totally prohibited me from thinking of you as just a friend. But here we are doing the friendship deal again. I guess. Right?" Justin said, knowing that the last string of sentences made little sense.

"Right."

"And it feels good to be friends like this." Justin looked at the watch clipped to his belt loop. "I wonder where Clipper is. You called him didn't you?"

"Well, I tried to call him but . . ."

"You didn't call him?"

"I just wanted to talk to you. Alone. In the restaurant, of course."

"Really?"

"Really," Kandi said smiling. "I just didn't know how much of Clipper's observational humor I could endure when you and I have been so out of touch."

"And so you intentionally didn't call Clipper?" Justin smiled slightly. Since Kandi rarely diverted from plans, this surprised him. "And you did this so we could talk?" he asked in a puzzled tone.

"Right," Kandi said. They looked at each other in silence for a moment. "So, are we ready to go inside?" Kandi asked with a grin. "I don't think they offer curbside service."

Justin's eyes widened as if he had forgotten where he was. "Oh, sorry. Let's head on in. I thought maybe you had another revelation."

"I hope you aren't mad about the absence of a chaperone," Kandi said.

"Uh, no;" Justin said chuckling. "I won't start a food fight, I promise. I think we're safe."

"Good," Kandi replied, as they walked toward the entrance of the restaurant.

Kandi didn't have an agenda, but she did have a few things she wanted to say to Justin—things she couldn't say around Clipper or Autumn. The small talk ended by the time their entrees arrived.

"I don't understand it either," she said when he asked her about her short-lived relationship with Zack Galloway. "I still think he's a great guy. I suppose it only started because his persistence got the best of me. And I really wanted something different. I wanted to be around someone who didn't have any concept of what I'd been through," she said. "So Zack was in the right place at the right time."

"Really?" Justin asked with interest.

"What I mean is, you know all my secrets, and most of them are things I've tried to forget. I just needed a break."

"I'm sorry if I made you feel that way," Justin replied.

"Don't say that. Really, I don't want you to even think it had anything to do with you except that you knew about my dad's addictions, my rough start here in Indy, my weird relationship with my mom, just . . . well . . . everything. Everything that I wanted to run away from—you knew it all," Kandi finished as her eyes moistened. "But the more I crawled into this shelter from the truth, the more I realized what I was doing. I was trying to develop a new identity. But how can you do that when the person closest to you knows who you really are? How can you grow close to someone when you want to hide? And then I realized the relationship with Zack was an escape for me."

"So how did it end?" Justin asked.

"By a mutual understanding that the relationship wasn't going to go anywhere. We're still friends. In fact, it wasn't anything else. He's a funny guy, and he inspires me. He was so out there on the edge. He has a passion for life. He just expresses it in weird ways," Kandi said and waited for Justin's response.

Justin looked away. The conversation was at an uncomfortable roadblock for a moment. Finally he said, "So then there's us."

"Right," Kandi said as she looked at him, suddenly feeling nervous.

"What's the deal with us?" Justin, said resuming the conversation.

"I don't know. I just . . . well . . . I missed being around you, but I didn't want to call and cause you more confusion," Kandi said.

Justin glanced up at the hostess station. His mouth dropped.

"What?" Kandi said, noticing Justin's face.

"Guess who just walked in the door?"

Kandi turned around. "Zack?"

"And some girl," Justin added.

"That's definitely weird," Kandi said.

"Did you tell him where we were going?"

"NO! I hope you don't think I'd do something like that," Kandi said, defensively.

"OK. OK. I believe you, Kandi. I'm sorry it's just—"

"Weird, so weird," Kandi finished for him.

"So this is all just a coincidence," Justin said with a smile. "Do you think we ought to wave? Make it a double date or something? What's the girl's name? She's a sophomore, isn't she?"

"I think her name is Jill something," Kandi replied as she sat frozen in her seat after turning back around. "So what are they doing now?"

"Just standing there, waiting to be seated."

"Have they seen us?"

"No. Think I should wave them over?"

"What?" Kandi said, somewhat aghast by Justin's suggestion.

"Wave them over. Say hi to them. I mean, you said that you two are still friends," Justin said.

Kandi couldn't believe that Justin didn't want to grab her hand and escape with her out the fire exit.

"If I had invited Clipper and Autumn's entire debate team here, that would have been more bearable than eating with Zack," Kandi said, becoming a little perturbed with Justin.

"I thought it was over," Justin said.

"It *is* over, Dip!" Kandi said.

"Dip? Did you just call me Dip?"

"I'm sorry," Kandi said, still nervous.

"Last time someone called me Dip was in the third grade," Justin said.

"I said I'm sorry. I'm just a little furious right now. Maybe if we just—"

"Too late. Here they come."

"No."

"Yep."

Justin immediately turned on the charm, and Kandi followed suit.

"Hey, guys!" Justin said, greeting them.

Jill seemed as shocked as Kandi, but Zack didn't miss a beat. "Hey, wow! Kandi! Justin! This is so weird," Zack said as he stooped down to hug a tense and stiff Kandi. "I have to confess. I saw you two on the road tonight and had to stop and say hi."

The statement made Kandi's head swim. *Why am I not surprised?* she thought to herself, enraged by the forwardness that at one time had attracted her to Zack.

"I promise I won't keep you. Just wanted to say hi. Feels like I haven't seen either of you for a while. Everything cool?" Zack asked.

"Great," Justin said behind his casual facade.

"I have to say that I admire your courage. I didn't think anyone would have the guts to show for the 'See You at the Pole' thing after all those threats. Guess you heard the news. Pretty scary stuff."

"What news?" Justin asked frowning.

"About the bomb they found at that church," Zack said.

"What?" Justin asked, stunned.

"Yeah. They found a bomb. But it was already diffused when the police got there."

"Where'd they find it?" Justin said.

"At some church. Some small church," Zack said. "They said someone had been arrested, but they didn't give a name."

"I can't believe it," Justin said.

"Neither can anyone else. I guess the Man upstairs really does have control over the situation," Zack said. "Oops. I'm sorry, Jill. This is—"

"Jill. We know Jill," Kandi said politely.

"Hi, Kandi. Zack talks about you all the time."

"Really?" Justin said leaning forward a bit.

"We really need to spend some more time together—the three of us," Zack said, until Jill frowned. "I mean, the four of us."

"Let's do it," Justin said with his arms crossed.

"But not tonight," Kandi quickly inserted.

"No, of course not," Zack said, laughing. "Not tonight."

"It's great to see you, Kandi. I really admire your artwork. I love that oil painting that's displayed in the art wing," Jill offered with a shy smile.

"Thanks," Kandi said, now feeling guilty for being such a party pooper.

"What's good here?" Zack asked Justin.

"It's all good," Justin said, still in shock from the news about the bomb.

"Great. I'll make sure we give you two some space," Zack said, winking at Justin and then walking away with Jill.

"I think we should box our food and see what Clipper knows about this bomb thing," Justin said.

"Sure," Kandi said. "I can't believe him. That is so Zack," Kandi said. "He sees us on the road and follows us, just so that he can reaffirm his own existence."

"Give him a break. I think that went pretty well," Justin said.

"Of course it went well. We're friends. F-R-I-E-N-D-S," Kandi said.

"Oh, really?" Justin said amusingly.

"I love you like a brother, but sometimes you really annoy me," Kandi said.

"That's what brothers do," Justin said with a laugh.

"I don't want my grandmother to come down here. You understand? I didn't do this! I'm trying to tell you, but you're not listening," A. C. yelled as he paced the conference room.

Detective Marty Fuller sat unemotional, his arms folded across his massive chest. Fuller intimidated most offenders. The veteran policeman was 45. He stood 6'3" and weighed over 280 pounds. He looked sternly at A. C., wanting him to know this arrest was not a game. "The evidence against you piles high. Don't be stupid, Andrew. Tell us the truth," he said.

"Don't call me that. I told you the last time I was in here not to call me that," A. C. sneered.

"I'll call you anything I want until you come clean. This isn't a small offense—an ounce of weed in your locker, son. We're talking attempted murder," the detective said.

"Do you think I'm stupid enough to plant a bomb with its wires cut in a church? Why would I want to do that?"

"Don't know. You tell me. Tell me that the fingerprints they just lifted off of it aren't yours," the detective said.

"I told you. I cut the wires. I sabotaged the plan," A. C. said angrily.

"Whose plan?" Detective Fuller asked.

"You figure it out," A. C. said.

"You're not in a position to protect anyone, A. C.!" the detective said louder, slamming his fist on the table in front of him.

"I'm not a snitch," A. C. replied.

"No, you're a liar and a bum! You're treating this like making a bomb was some kind of a game. Well, it wasn't. People could have been killed today, and you say you know who's responsible and you won't tell me," the detective said, now fuming with anger. "You're a coward, A. C. You think we don't know what's going on here?"

Both of them were quiet for a few moments. A. C. struggled with the dilemma. He thought about the threats he'd received on his own life. He knew if he were on the other side of the jail walls, the small group of terrorist friends would track him down and every secret he withheld from the detectives would go with him to the grave. He hated being loyal to either side, but he knew he only had himself to blame for the situation he was in. After wrestling with the decision, A. C. made his choice and blurted, "His name is Elliot. You know an Elliot?"

The detective didn't respond to A. C.'s revelation. He scribbled something on his pad, rose to his feet, and walk to the door. "Lock him up," he mumbled to the jailer. And then he turned back to A. C., "We'll talk more later."

"Wait! Hold on. What are you doing? I just gave you a name!" A. C. said angrily.

"Get some rest. And get used to your cell. Chances are you'll be there awhile," the detective said. "By the way, I understand tomorrow's your eighteenth birthday. Happy birthday. You mess with me after tomorrow, and I'll charge you as an adult. I'll make sure you aren't free for another five to fifteen years."

"I really don't think you should get yourself involved in that, Clip," Mr. Hayes said. "That's something Jenny and her parents are going to have to work out on their own."

His dad's negative reaction to his suggestion of another way to help his friend Jenny Elton in Louisville startled him. Clipper had been Jenny's only support during the past few months. Her parents had practically abandoned her as an outcast after discovering she was pregnant. Jenny was filled with remorse over the unwise choice to get sexually involved with an old boyfriend. One night of sex had completely devastated her life, especially since her parents were more concerned about the family's reputation than their daughter's well-being. Clipper laid awake nights wondering how they could be so cruel. He still couldn't understand how they could have encouraged an abortion to save that reputation. Jenny had decided to keep the child, and her parents had rewarded that decision by shunning her. Clipper wanted to help her parents see how she needed them.

"But Dad, that's just it—she can't talk to her parents about it. They won't listen," Clipper replied.

"Then what makes you think they'll listen to you if they won't listen to their own daughter?"

"I don't know," said Clipper, digging the toe of his tennis shoe into the carpet. "I just can't stand the thought of Jenny lying there in that hospital in Louisville all alone. She ought to be here with her family and friends!"

"Well, I'm not going to tell you what to do on this one. You're old enough to decide for yourself. But I will tell you that I don't think it's a good idea," Mr. Hayes said as he walked out of Clipper's room.

Clipper sat staring at his floor, or at least what little he could see of it peeking through the scattered clothes and papers. He knew his father was probably right, *But somebody's got to stand up for Jenny!* he thought.

Even after he'd found out about Jenny's pregnancy by another guy, Clipper still loved her. He'd even considered marrying her so she could keep her baby. But they'd both realized that as young as they were, this would only make matters worse. Still, he cared for her deeply and felt very protective of her.

"What have I got to lose?" Clipper said aloud to his Michael Jordan poster. "I mean, it's not like I could make matters any worse than they already are."

Clipper reached for the phone and dialed the Elton household. As brave as he tried to be, his stomach was doing somersaults while he waited for someone to answer. After a couple of rings, Mrs. Elton picked up the phone.

"Hello, Mrs. Elton? This is Clipper Hayes, Jenny's friend."

There was a long pause and then Mrs. Elton said, "Yes, Clipper, I remember you."

"Um, I just wanted to call and see how Jenny was doing. I mean, I know she's in the hospital, and I was just wondering—"

"She's fine, Clipper," Mrs. Elton cut him off.

"That's good," Clipper's confidence quickly ebbed. "Well, tell Jenny I asked about her next time you talk to her, OK?"

"I'll be sure and do that. Goodbye, Clipper," Mrs. Elton hung up the phone before Clipper could say more.

Way to go, Mr. Hero! Clipper thought to himself. *That was real smooth. You really helped Jenny a ton! What a loser!* Clipper kicked a couple of piles of clothes around. In doing so, he unearthed one of the letters Jenny had written him. He reached down and picked it up, inhaling the soft fragrance of her stationery, somewhat mixed with the odor of his musty gym clothes.

With resolve, Clipper picked up the phone and dialed Jenny's mother again.

"Hello?" Mrs. Elton answered the second time.

"Mrs. Elton? Hi, it's Clipper Hayes again. Look, I'm sorry for bothering you, but there was something else I really needed to talk to you about."

"Yes, I'm waiting," Mrs. Elton said, irritation creeping into her voice.

"It's about Jenny. Would you please let her . . . I mean, is there any way you'd consider . . . I think she'd be much better off . . ."

"Clipper, what on earth are you trying to say?" demanded Mrs. Elton.

"Couldn't you find it in your heart to forgive Jenny and let her come back home?" Clipper finally blurted out.

Mrs. Elton sat in shocked silence for so long that Clipper thought perhaps she had hung up on him.

"Hello, Mrs. Elton?" he asked.

"I'm here," she whispered. "Clipper, I know you care about Jenny a great deal, so I'm going to try to not be angry with you for this. But the fact of the matter is, it's none of your business. This has been a very difficult time for all of us, and Jenny's father and I agree that this is what's best."

"For who? You or Jenny?" Clipper couldn't help but ask.

"For all of us!" Mrs. Elton retorted. "Now, Clipper, I'm not going to discuss this with you any further." Clipper could hear her voice choking up with emotion. "Jenny's my daughter, and I love her. But . . . for right now, this is what's best. I've got to go. Goodbye." And with that, Clipper was left once again with a dial tone.

He sat on the floor on top of some socks and underwear with a dejected look. *Well, Jenny, at least I tried.*

A few minutes later, the phone began to ring. *Probably Mrs. Elton calling to ream me out,* thought Clipper. He decided to let one of his parents answer it. Mr. Hayes stuck his head in Clipper's room. "Phone's for you," he said.

"Could you take a message?" Clipper asked.

"I think you better take this one. It's the police," his dad said with a look of concern on his face.

Clipper rushed to the police station at their request. He dreaded going, but he wanted to know why they needed him as soon as possible. He walked in and was directed to Detective

Fuller's office. Detective Fuller glanced at Clipper, and then returned to the computer screen where he scrolled through a spreadsheet of some kind while chewing on a coffee stirrer.

"You Clifford Hayes?" Fuller asked.

"Yes, sir," Clipper replied.

"Friends call you Clipper?"

"Yes."

"Clip?"

"I'm sorry?" Clipper asked, confused.

"I said, friends also call you Clip?"

"Oh, sorry. Yes. I didn't—"

"Do you know about this group they call The Association?" Fuller asked finally, swiveling around to face Clipper.

"I've corresponded with some of them," Clipper said carefully.

"What do you mean by corresponded with them?" Fuller asked.

"They've E-mailed me on occasion and—"

"'Scuse me son," Fuller said holding an open palm out to Clipper as he grabbed the phone. "Kelly? Can you hunt down Jackson. I need him to pick something up at this boy's house."

"I don't understand," Clipper said.

"We need your computer. You *will* let us hold on to it for a couple of days. I can always ask for a search warrant," Fuller said casually.

"No. That's OK. I just have some stuff that I need for school that—"

"No problem. After you and I are done, Lieutenant Jackson'll escort you to your house, and you can put what you need on a disk. That sound all right?"

"Let me get this straight. You're taking my computer?" Clipper asked, confused.

"Yes, for a couple of days. I think I heard you say that you're letting us take it to retrieve information that may be vital to our case. Now if you refuse, I'll just file for a search warrant. Your choice," Fuller said.

"OK. Fine," Clipper said. His mouth dried up from nervousness as his heart raced. "Do you think I'm a part of this whole bombing incident?" Clipper asked.

"We don't know that," Fuller said. "If you're innocent, you have nothing to hide. So tell me about A. C. Is he a member?" he asked.

"I couldn't say," Clipper said.

"Couldn't or won't say?" Fuller replied.

"I don't know, sir. I think maybe at some time he was. But he never came right out and said anything definite. He just hinted around," Clipper said.

"You knew they were planning to bomb, right?" Fuller said.

"Everyone knew. It was on the news," Clipper said defensively.

"I'm not talking about the news. I'm talking about inside information," Fuller clarified.

"No. I had no inside information at all," Clipper said as he digested the implications of this meeting.

"But they talked to you personally. You even went to a party last month that this group put together. Skull's Bluff? Is that what they call that place?"

"Yes. I went because I was trying to help straighten A. C. out," Clipper replied.

"Straighten him out? Why?"

Clipper's mind went totally blank. He didn't know how to answer. Finally he said, "Because I thought that's what God wanted me to do."

Fuller chuckled. "I've heard lots of alibis, but that's one for the ages, kid. God told you to . . . He told you to go get smashed at some wild campout. What religion are you?"

"I didn't get drunk, sir! You don't understand," Clipper said angrily.

"We'll finish this conversation later. Jackson will follow you home," Fuller said gesturing to the door.

"But hold on a second. I haven't been able to explain a single thing," Clipper said in desperation.

"I don't need any more information now. If I need you, we'll talk later."

A. C. jerked up when he heard the sound of keys. The jailer opened the door and ordered A. C. to come with him.

"What time is it?" A. C. asked.

"It's 10 P.M."

"I told you I don't want to see anybody."

"Then close your eyes," the jailer said and chuckled at his own joke. The jailer cuffed him and took him into the visitor's booth. To his surprise, A. C. saw Clipper sitting on the other end of the glassed-in visitors' room. "What are you doing here?"

"Two hours ago I would have asked the same question. The real question is: What have you been saying to these guys?" Clipper asked seriously.

"I don't get it," A. C. replied.

"Why did I just get grilled by the police about the St. Luke's bomb discovery? What did you tell them?" Clipper said.

"I didn't tell them anything," A. C. said.

"They've looked at my phone records. They took my computer from the house. My mom's about to go totally mental. Dad's out there in the lobby. I don't even want to think about what he's gonna say to me on the way home," Clipper said angrily.

"That's the way these guys work," A. C. replied. "They feel like they didn't get enough information from me, so they start jacking with the people that they know I associate with, which happens to include you. Remember, I am one of your little missionary projects," A. C. said sarcastically.

"Flush the attitude, A. C. What did you tell them?"

"I didn't tell them anything. Believe me. If they really thought you were involved, you'd be in here with me," A. C. said.

"I think you have a little more of a rap sheet than I do."

"Is that why you came here? To blame me for losing your computer?" A. C. asked.

"No, I just don't get why you're being so closemouthed about everything. You're gonna have to start talking," Clipper said.

"They wouldn't listen to me even if I tried to tell my story."

"And what *is* your story?" Clipper asked.

"My story is simple. I didn't do it. In fact, I'm the one who disengaged the bomb."

"You what?!"

"The bomb at St. Luke's. I cut the wires and split."

Clipper eyebrows raised in disbelief. "Why didn't you just call the police. You could have gotten killed."

"If I had called the police, the building would have been toast. There wasn't any time to call. I knew when it was set to blow and—"

Clipper interrupted A. C. and held his hands out like he didn't want to hear any more. "That's crazy. You're telling me you knew it would happen? Where it would happen? And you just changed your mind and decided to pull the plug?"

"Take it or leave it. That's what happened," A. C. said.

"Did you tell them I had nothing to do with it?"

"I had a two-minute drill of questions and to tell the truth, Clipper, your name never came up. Even if it did, your reputation wouldn't be my first priority. Just when I agreed to give them a name—not yours by the way—the detective said he had heard enough and walked out."

"That's weird," Clipper said.

"I'm going before the judge tomorrow to plead. The strange thing about this is, for the first time in my life, I really do care. I grew a conscience, and it's freaking me out. I'm scared about what'll happen," A. C. said. He looked away from Clipper. The emotions of the past few hours surfaced. He wanted to cry, and he wasn't sure he could hold it back. His hands trembled under the stress.

After a long silence A. C. continued. "Tomorrow I turn eighteen. I'm an adult. Some birthday. The detective said they'll try to bring me in as an adult."

"You told me you were sixteen," Clipper responded.

"I lied. But the system doesn't," A. C. said. "I thought maybe if I could stop this that I'd have a chance at a normal life. I wanted a normal life," A. C. said and then smiled. "God has a sick sense of humor if you ask me. I decide to make a break for normality, and then He slams me."

"That's not His plan," Clipper said solemnly.

"Oh, yeah? How do you know that?" A. C. asked in anger.

"He says, 'I know the plans I have for you. Plans to build you up. Not to tear you down. Plans to give you a future and a hope,'" Clipper said awkwardly.

"Another quote from the Bible genius, I assume," A. C. said, feeling his rebellious nature rise up again.

"I'm not trying to be a geek about this. You just have to tell the truth, A. C. Making truth work is a heck of a lot easier than trying to make alibis and finding loopholes. All you have to do is tell them what you know."

"It might be too late to start working on the truth. They don't trust me, and they're looking for an easy target to pin this on. Don't you see that?" A. C. responded.

"I'm not gonna let that happen to you," Clipper said earnestly.

"As if you have any power to keep that promise. I'm a lost cause."

"You're not," Clipper shot back.

"Shut up, Clipper. You don't know anything about me."

"I don't need to know anything about you," Clipper said calmly. "God can change anyone."

"Maybe God works for you and your nice Brady Bunch family, big house with the three-car garage, but it won't work for me. I was destined for this."

"But—"

"I really wish you'd leave me alone, Clipper," A. C. said as he stood up and knocked on the door to signal he was ready to leave the visitation room.

The audience stood to their feet and applauded at the end of Summit High theatre's first production. Zack played the lead in an absurdist comedy, and no other student actor rivaled his talent. He performed like a New York actor. Justin fought a twinge of jealousy as he stood with Kandi and Autumn, applauding. He wondered if the Zack/Kandi relationship was really over. But still he tried his best just to put the whole mess out of his mind.

"Wow, that was incredible," Kandi said as they exited the theatre. "How do they memorize all those lines about nothing. I mean, it wasn't like the show had some plot or meaning."

"Guess that's why they call it 'theatre of the absurd,'" Justin said wryly.

"That's definitely the correct category," Autumn said seriously. "What's the redeeming value in a couple eating dinner and speaking gibberish? Is this what our society has come to? We're glorifying a lack of meaning."

"Actually, Autumn, it was just a play. It's supposed to be entertainment," Kandi said.

"I still don't get it. I have a hard time with people who think life doesn't have any meaning," Autumn said.

"That's the whole point. I think the entire human condition invokes a deep sense of existential, how shall I say, residue outside the standard paradigm of the Judeo-Christian faith," Justin said in mock seriousness.

Autumn stopped walking. "Are you making fun of me?" she asked.

The three laughed, until they heard someone call to them. "Hey, guys! Thanks for coming!" Zack shouted through the mass of exiting theatre patrons. His strange formal black-tie costume seemed even more out of place without the aid of stage lighting. "I didn't know you were going to be here. I'm honored."

"That was incredible," Kandi said. "How long has the club been working on that?"

"We began a couple weeks before school started. I love absurdist theatre. It's more realistic," Zack joked as he twirled his top hat in his hands.

Justin chimed in politely, "It was great. I'm extremely impressed. I think you really have a future in this."

Zack's eyes lit up. "Hey! Where are you three going now?"

Autumn looked at Kandi and Justin and then said, "We hadn't really planned—"

"Then why don't you come to the cast party? It'll be a blast," Zack said.

Autumn, Justin, and Kandi looked at each other.

"Sounds fun," Kandi said, shrugging her shoulders.

Justin felt his defensiveness rise once more. "Sure. Love to," he lied, pasting a smile on his face.

Kandi looked at Justin strangely.

"Here's the address. It's on Summit Boulevard. The big, brick house," Zack said as he scribbled the info down on a scrap of paper he had in his pocket. "I promise I'll be there, but you might not recognize me—I won't be wearing makeup and a top hat."

As the three friends sat in the front seat of Justin's car on the way to the party, Kandi began to grow nervous about the potential awkwardness of the situation. "Are you sure you want to go?" Kandi asked Justin.

"Sure, I'm sure. I said yes too, of my own free will," Justin replied, looking straight ahead with a subtle smile plastered on his face.

"You aren't trying to prove anything are you?"

"Prove anything?" Justin asked, sounding distant.

"Proving that you trust me around a guy I dated a couple of times," Kandi said.

"Ha! That's a laugh. I don't have anything to prove, Kandi girl. I'm fine. I think Zack's a pretty OK kind of guy. I mean you still think he's fine," Justin said. He then corrected the dangling implication. "I mean that he's—oh, you know what I mean."

Autumn quickly blurted out, "Great night, huh? Super weather. Love this weather we're having. Really nice, huh?"

When they pulled into the drive and opened the door, they could hear the music through the walls of the house.

"I guess we can negate the hopes of avoiding hearing impairment for a few days," Autumn said.

"Loosen up. You might enjoy it. It's called 'hip-hop,'" Justin said.

"I *know* what hip-hop is Justin. I'm not *that* out of it." Autumn rolled her eyes and opened the door.

Jill Welch greeted them with a smile beaming from ear to ear as they walked through the front door. Her light-blonde hair and svelte frame made her stand out in the crowd. "Come on in! I heard you guys were coming. Great!"

"What?" Kandi asked over the blaring music.

"I SAID COME IN! GLAD YOU'RE HERE!"

"THANKS!" Kandi yelled back as politely as possible.

A mass of students crammed into the large living room of the house. Some were dancing, some eating and joking around. Others attempted to communicate by screaming into each other's ears. Justin, Autumn, and Kandi grabbed a few munchies and watched the mayhem quietly. Kandi wondered what Justin thought about the party. It all seemed kosher to her. No beer. No weird stuff. No couples sneaking into closets. But for some reason Kandi felt uncomfortable being at a party with Justin at Zack's invitation. She grabbed Justin's hand and said to him and Autumn, "Let's go."

A few seconds after they walked out Zack popped out of the house and called out, "Hey guys. Wait up!"

"Hey, Zack," Autumn began. "We didn't want to be rude and make a big deal out of leaving early so we—"

"Great! Go ahead leave me in there suffering from a sub-woofer-induced migraine. Don't worry about me, I'll just stay out here on the porch and reflect on the lonely life of a penniless actor," Zack said straight-faced.

"And so you saved your best performance for the cast party," Autumn said coyly.

"Ouch. That hurt. Gonna take me awhile to recover from that one. I should know never to try to pull one over on the debate babe," Zack said. "Hey, I've got an idea. I want to show you something."

"What?" Justin asked.

"It's kind of my secret place. Never shown it to anyone else," Zack said, trying to add some mystery to his lure.

"Oooooooh. A secret place . . ." Justin replied facetiously. "You haven't even shown it to Kandi?"

"Shut up!" Kandi exclaimed. She didn't see the humor in Justin's question.

"Definitely not. She didn't stay around long enough. Kandi found out what I'm really like and ran back to her old flame," Zack said.

"That's it. Let's get out of here," Kandi replied.

"I was joking, Kandi. We're friends! Come on. You don't have to take everything so seriously," Zack said.

"So where is this secret place?" Autumn asked.

"Follow old Raffiki. He knows the way," Zack said, imitating the voice of *The Lion King* monkey. "It's only a short drive. Away from this mayhem!"

"It's early. Whadayasay?" Justin asked the two girls.

"Definitely not," Kandi said under her breath.

"I'm curious," Justin said.

Autumn added, "I'm skeptical. He seems a little . . ."

"Hyper?" Kandi asked.

"Right," Autumn said.

Zack, still out of earshot of their comments, yelled out to them, "I'll go kidnap Jill. It'll be fun. Strictly G-rated entertainment—appropriate for all audiences." He sidestepped back inside, leaving Autumn, Kandi, and Justin staring at each other now, feeling obligated to go.

"He's not drunk," Justin said.

"I think he's a little too hyper to be drunk," Autumn said.

"That's just Zack. He's like this. Give him a minute, and he'll take an hour," Kandi said.

After a moment Zack reappeared carrying Jill in his arms. "Zack! Are you nuts!" she screamed.

"Me Zack. *You* nuts. Zack and Jill went up the hill and the others came tumbling after. I've always wanted to date a Jill. Our two names together are really funny. Don't you agree?" he laughed.

"He's a certified idiot," Jill explained. "He gets this way after performances. You should have seen him last night."

"Tomorrow and tomorrow and tomorrow," Zack said in a Shakespearean voice. "Yesterday, all my troubles seemed so far away. Wait, that's not Shakespeare. That's McCartney."

Zack threw Jill into the car and sped off to the end of the driveway where they waited while Autumn, Justin, and Kandi found their car and followed with more than a little skepticism.

"So what do you make of all this?" Justin asked the girls.

"I'd say he's probably the most extroverted, so-unlike-Kandi guy I know," Autumn said winking at Justin.

"I'll take that as a compliment," Kandi interjected.

"Is he always like this?" Autumn asked.

"Actually his personality seems to have intensified," Kandi replied.

"He's probably still burning off the energy from the play," Justin suggested.

"I think it's more than that," Autumn replied. "Do you have any idea where we're going?"

"Not a clue," Justin said.

Kandi shook her head.

They soon had gone from the highway to a country road and finally to a narrow gravel road.

"Have you ever been out here?" Kandi asked Justin.

"Nope," Justin replied.

"One more mile down this road, and I say we head back," Autumn said.

"OK. One more mile."

A moment later Zack veered his car over to the side of the road and slowed it to a stop. The moonless night accented the allure of the unfamiliar territory. Kandi's heart raced, wondering if it they might have missed a "no trespassing" sign. Justin parked a few feet behind Zack. Before he had shifted into park, Jill and Zack were already jumping over a small fence. Autumn, Kandi, and Justin looked at each other and followed the glow of Zack's flashlight.

Zack took Jill's hand and pulled her along, and as he did, she laughed hysterically.

"You don't have a flashlight?" Kandi asked as they followed.

"I really wasn't expecting to be hiking tonight. I wonder if we're still in Indiana?" Justin asked.

"That's not funny," Autumn said breathlessly.

"I just hope you know how to get back home," Kandi said to Justin.

"We're fine. It's early, and we're twenty minutes south of town. How hard can that be?"

The three slowed down when Zack stopped about twenty yards ahead of them.

"I'll do it. I'll jump," he said in a threatening voice.

"What?" Autumn asked.

"I'll jump, and don't try to stop me!"

Autumn looked over at Justin and gasped, "It's a cliff!"

"Cut it out, Zack," Kandi said, thinking that this was surely another one of Zack's pranks.

"I'm gonna do it. Everyone hates me! Don't lie to me. You talk about me. I coulda been somebody! I coulda been a contender! Somebody stop me!"

A moment later Zack fell backwards off the cliff. A splash soon followed. Instinctively Justin followed him in. Kandi and Autumn ran to the edge, but they couldn't see anything. Then they heard Zack laughing and Justin reacting to the cold dark water.

"Are you crazy!" Justin shouted at Zack.

"Certified, man," Zack said, still laughing. "Is this great or what? Come on in, girls."

Autumn and Kandi simultaneously shouted back, "No!"

"Don't be a stick-in-the-mud! It's great—this is what life's all about! C'mon!"

Kandi yelled to Justin, "Are you coming back?"

"Mama's calling . . ." Zack mocked.

"I'll be there in a second," Justin said.

"You're going home with us," Autumn stated to Jill.

"I don't know. I think it looks kind of fun," Jill replied.

After a few minutes Justin climbed the rocky walls of the quarry pit to where the girls were. His teeth chattered as he spoke. "Let's get out of here."

"What about you, Jill?" Kandi asked.

"I think I'll stay," Jill said. "He's so cute. I mean, how many times do you get to meet someone so—"

"Crazy?" Autumn proposed.

"No," Jill said, sounding a little offended, "so adventuresome."

Zack yelled up to Jill. "I'm coming up. I've got a towel in the trunk."

"He planned this," Justin said under his breath to Kandi.

"Like I said, he just loves being on the edge," Jill said to them.

"Or rather over," Autumn added.

"I love him," Jill confessed with a beaming smile.

Autumn, Justin, and Kandi looked at each other in disbelief.

"So I guess that means you'll be staying here with Zack," Justin said.

Jill nodded. Justin, Kandi, and Autumn got in the car and drove back. Justin concentrated on retracing the route back to civilization. Once they got back on the main road, he interrupted the silence. "I'm freezing. Tell me again why we followed that lunatic?"

"It was your choice, Justin," Kandi said.

"I can't believe you ever went out with him," Justin said. "I thought he was really going to kill himself. What kind of a sick person would joke around like that?"

"Please don't go there," Kandi said as she burned with embarrassment.

"Fine . . . Fine . . . I'm sorry," Justin said after a moment. "Anyone mind if I turn up the heat?"

As soon as Justin got home, he called Clipper. He was concerned because Clipper seemed to be constructing walls between himself and his best friends. He wouldn't admit it, but Justin could tell.

"So how was the play?" Clipper asked.

"Weird. How are you doing?"

"Well, let's see . . . Jenny's parents think I'm some nosey little weasel trying to tell them what to do. The police grilled me, trying to squeeze information out of me about the bomb. I'd say it just goes to show that I'm a busybody, disturbed, pompous terrorist who just happens to be an active member of Grove Community Church."

Justin laughed.

"It's not funny, Justin," Clipper said angrily. "What good does it do to try to help people? What good does it do to take risks, or to do what you think God expects you to do?" Clipper asked.

"Nobody said it would be easy to follow God, Clip."

"Yeah, but shouldn't there be some progress?" Clipper asked.

"You are totally forgetting something," Justin said.

"Forgetting what?" Clipper said.

"Forgetting that if you hadn't developed a friendship with A. C., chances are St. Luke's would be a pile of rubble."

"You don't know that," Clipper said.

"You're forgetting that Jenny might have had an abortion. You're not thinking logically. What do you expect, Clipper?"

Clipper didn't respond for a moment finally he said, "Gotta go."

"Why?"

"I just do, Justin. Would you please back off? Sheesh!"

With the jailer at his side, A. C. grew anxious as he walked into the small conference room at the county courthouse with his hands cuffed and his feet shackled. He saw his grandmother, Mrs. Cushman, and a man who looked to be in his sixties sitting on the opposite side of a battered oak table. Mrs. Cushman, obviously devastated by her grandson's situation, had been crying. Her eyes were red and her stress manifested itself in a slight tremble. She had been the sole guardian of A. C. for years. A. C. had never known his mother.

A. C. walked in, sat down, and focused his eyes on the scarred tabletop.

The jailer spoke up, "I'll be watching from the monitor just outside the door. Knock on the door when you're finished, and I'll take him back."

After the jailer exited the conference room, Mrs. Cushman spoke first. "What is this, Andrew?" she asked, her voice shaking with emotion.

"It's just my luck," he stated, still looking down and drumming his fingers on the table. "Who's this?" he asked looking up at the man.

"This is the court-appointed lawyer, Mr. Luffman," she replied.

Mr. Luffman cleared his throat, loosened his collar, and began without a greeting, "In about thirty minutes you are going to be arraigned, and I need to know if you are willing to allow me to negotiate a plea bargain."

"A plea bargain?! You haven't even asked me if I did anything," A. C. said angrily.

"The evidence against you stacks up rather nicely, son," Mr. Luffman said assertively.

"I want another lawyer," A. C. demanded.

"I think I'm giving you the best counsel," Mr. Luffman replied.

"You're telling me to roll over and play dead. That's the *best* counsel you've got? I'm telling you that I'm innocent."

Mr. Luffman opened his briefcase and spread five legal-sized sheets of paper on the table. "Fingerprints on the bomb, fake ID, receipts from a gun show, a few incriminating phone calls last summer. It doesn't exactly make you look like a choirboy. If you have any involvement with this incident, I think you should consider a plea-bargain agreement. The prosecutor is anxious to get this case off the docket and get a plea. If you plead no contest, you'll do time in a juvenile detention center. If this thing goes to trial, the judge may decide to try you as an adult, and I promise you, nobody in this room wants that, especially you. The media is going to have a field day with this story. We're talking live coverage. Your future will be shot."

"It already is," A. C. said.

"And I'll be hard-pressed to seat a jury that won't be screaming for blood. This year has been terrible. We've had over twenty kids killed in shootings on school campuses, not to mention all the churches that have been destroyed. I think we should consider a plea bargain. Sooner or later you'll have to face the fact that the best thing you can do is settle this thing without a jury."

"What happened, Andrew?" Mrs. Cushman finally asked.

"It's a long story, and I don't want to go into the whole thing right now," replied A. C. "But I'm not the villain. I'm the hero. Of course my prints are all over the place. I was the one who disarmed the bomb."

"How did you know how to do that?" his grandmother demanded.

"Because I helped make the bomb," A. C. said loudly.

"Please," Mr. Luffman said. "Hold your voice down. This is exactly what I mean when I talk about the jeopardy of this case," he said in a soft, yet tense voice. "You have to use your head and listen to the options I'm giving you."

"I'll NEVER say that I was responsible," A. C. said through clenched teeth.

"Fine then. We'll take it one step at a time."

As Mr. Luffman explained the proceedings of the arraignment, A. C.'s mind kept returning to the thought of the punishment he would face in a state prison if the judicial system found him guilty of attempted murder. He thought of the stories he had heard of life inside the steel walls—stories of rape, unsolved murders, and maddening months, even years of loneliness. Hopelessness and fear engulfed him.

After the meeting he walked outside to the courthouse, blinded by the light of the early fall sun. An onslaught of the local news media crowded toward him. For an instant, he thought about covering his face. Hopelessness kept his hands clasped in front of him. There was no reason to hide. Moments later, he stood before the judge, straight-faced and unresponsive. He had to be prompted by Mr. Luffman to enter the plea of not guilty. He thought to himself, *If I ever get out of here and away from all these eyes, I'll kill myself.*

Amid the normal fracas in the school hall on Monday morning, Kandi heard someone call her name. She turned around and saw Melissa, the Summit High gossip queen who always had an interesting and not entirely accurate version of everything that happened at the school. Some students accused her of bugging phones and hiring detectives. Her ability to dig out information and add her own personal twist made her a person to be dreaded if not feared.

"How's it goin', girl?"

"Hey, Melissa. What's going on?"

"If anyone should know, I should. I heard that you and Justin are together again. Talk about a complete turnaround! Runnin' hot and cold these days?"

"Melissa, we've always been friends even when we weren't dating. No big deal. We're not quote/unquote dating. We're just friends."

"Hear you went on a little excursion with him and Zack to some kind of lake last night," Melissa said as she flashed a devilish look at Kandi.

"That's funny, Melissa," Kandi said as she opened her locker.

"How weird is that? You date Zacky baby and then take Justin on a double date with Jill and Zack. Weird, weird, weird," Melissa said and then clicked the roof of her mouth a few times with her tongue.

"It really wasn't all that weird. But before I explain the whole thing to you would you mind telling me—"

"Jill. She told me the whole story. You know, I think she's really falling for Zack. Kind of like you did."

"Did not. We went out twice. I wouldn't exactly call that falling for someone," Kandi said defensively.

"Oh, whatever."

"Hello girls," Jill said as she walked up to Melissa and Kandi.

"Speaking of . . . Is this a coincidence or what?" Melissa said. "Isn't she just a doll? Isn't she? So like, are you in love?"

Jill simply smiled and lifted her eyebrows.

"See. What did I say?" Melissa said ribbing Kandi with her elbow as she folded a stick of gum into her mouth.

"He's just so full of excitement," Jill chattered. "I never know what's going to happen next. Every day he surprises me with another side of himself. He's just so—"

"Skitzo?" Melissa said and then laughed heartily. "Look, I gotta go. Going to have to beg Miss Bad-breath Bunson to let me make up the exam I missed last week."

Melissa left Jill and Kandi staring at each other for a second until Kandi broke the silence. "So how long did the two of you stay out there?"

"Long enough for him to convince me to jump in and for me to just about die of hypothermia," Jill said smiling and bouncing on her heels slightly. "We swam. Totally innocent. He's sure a polite . . . uh, nut."

"That's an interesting way to describe it," Kandi said.

"I don't know. I just think he has such an incredible future," Jill said.

"As long as he doesn't end up as a quadriplegic from taking chances like he did last night," Kandi said skeptically.

"He's done that a thousand times. That's his place to get away. He has the quarry memorized," Jill said.

"Let me ask you something—and I really don't want to upset you or anything but—doesn't it seem like his moods fluctuate a lot?"

"Oh, Kandi, that's just him. He's an actor."

"It's different than being an actor. At times I've seen him on this incredible high and then the bottom would just fall out. It was weird. And it's more than just being really happy or energized. He's super-hyper and talks so fast sometimes that it makes my head spin. Do you think he's . . . ," Kandi stopped, really hoping that Jill would know where she was going and fill in the blank.

"That he's what?" Jill asked, oblivious to Kandi's leading.

"Well, the only time I've ever seen someone that hyper, it was, um, you know, with a little outside help." Kandi said and then braced herself.

"You think he's on drugs, don't you? I can't believe you said that. Of course he's not taking anything. People with his kind of talent don't need drugs. He's stronger than that, Kandi. What do you think he's taking?" Jill said in disbelief.

"I don't know. I'm just concerned," Kandi said, backing away slightly.

"Don't be concerned. You know, Zack was right. He warned me you might accuse him of something like this. You're as paranoid as they come," Jill said.

"So that's what Zack thinks?" Kandi said, somewhat hurt by the revelation.

"I think you're jealous that I'm having such a great relationship with him—something you obviously couldn't maintain. He's not on drugs, so get that thought out of your head. He's the most affectionate, most upbeat guy I've ever met, so just forget about it. And by all means, don't say things like that around Melissa the Mouth." Jill shook her head in disgust and walked away.

A. C. stared at the walls of his cell and wondered how long he'd be surrounded by the sound of heavy iron doors, the constant barrage of arguments, and the stench. The smell of heavy-duty floor wax and deodorizer became as sickening to him as the smell of the new kids who stumbled into their cells drunk and disoriented.

He grew tired of listening to them plead with their parents on the telephone to come and get them out. He knew they hated their parents just as much as he hated his. He hated his mother because she never claimed him. His father only returned to his grandmother's house when he needed money or when he'd been kicked out of apartments and halfway houses. It left A. C. with more than just a feeling of worthlessness. It left him feeling like he didn't even exist.

In the cell, he slept sporadically and with more than a little fear. Every night he experienced nightmares about the past—his anger, his alcoholic father, the abuse, the rejection, and the hopelessness that followed him. He dreamed about his experimentation with huffing, acid, cocaine, and sex.

But the nightmares of his future haunted him even more. He dreamed of being tortured and executed by the group with whom he had plotted terror. He woke up in the middle of the night, his pillow drenched with sweat, dreaming of life in a prison, where every remaining thread of dignity and desire for life would be stripped from him. A. C. felt that years in prison would reduce him to being a shell, a soulless zombie. *But,* he thought, *what's the difference? I'm already that zombie.*

Sometimes the stress and mental anguish became so terrifying that it felt like ants were crawling through his brain. He wished he could write, but they wouldn't let him use a pen or pencil in his cell without supervision, and he knew he couldn't write knowing that the guard would monitor every move he made. Several times he thought about praying, but why would God listen to him? And why would he want to talk to this God anyway? This God who let his life turn out like this. No, he wouldn't pray. At least not yet. Perhaps not ever.

"A. C.? Detective Fuller's here. He wants to talk."

"Finally," A. C. replied, shaking his head in disgust. The officer unlocked his cell and took him back to the conference room where Detective Fuller sat. The detective didn't look up from his pad when A. C. walked in and sat down. Fuller's indifferent demeanor agitated A. C.

"Luffman's not here. You OK with that?" Fuller asked, still scribbling.

"I told you I don't give a rip about the court-appointed weasel in a monkey suit. I haven't done anything."

"Right. You've done a whole lot of nothin' since you moved to Indy," Fuller replied. "Elliot Anderson's the ring leader, huh?"

"No, Elliot Carter."

"Same guy."

"What?" A. C. asked, confused.

Fuller pushed his pad to the side and folded his hands in front of himself on the table.

"He's been calling himself Elliot Carter since he dropped out of high school three years ago in Bloomington. He's been involved in hate crimes, drug trafficking, petty theft. Spent some time in Ohio where he weaseled his way out of an attempted rape charge. You two are quite a pair. How long you known him?"

"Five or six months, I guess."

"What did you know about him when you met?" Fuller asked as he stuck the pen in his shirt pocket and loosened his tie.

"It's not like I do background checks on everybody I know, Fuller," A. C. said.

"Well, maybe you should have, cause I'm finding that whenever I check into leads on Elliot I practically trip over evidence that links you to the crime. I've got a better case on *you* than I do *him*." Fuller exhaled loudly and rubbed the bridge of his nose.

A. C. sat as the policeman slid his chair away from the table. The detective rubbed his forehead in aggravation. "My head is killing me. If I were you, I'd start talking because I am sick of this charade, A. C."

"I'm in danger. Don't you see that? I'm safer in here than I am out there," A. C. said.

"A. C., believe it or not, I'm not here to hang you. I just
want to find out the truth. Don't you see that? I'm listening, and
all you do is drop hints. So you don't like the lawyer. Fine. You
say you didn't do it. Fine. But you are facing time in the state
prison, which is certainly not a cakewalk. You'll deal with rape,
the dregs of society, gangs that make your little 'Association'
look like Boy Scouts. If I were you, I'd get Mr. Public Defender
What's-his-face in here immediately and give us something to
go on before this whole thing goes to trial."

Back in his cell later that evening, A. C. had time to pon-
der what Fuller had said. He knew if he didn't cooperate and
give the police department the information they wanted—all
the information—he would spend a great deal of his young
adulthood in prison. But he also knew Elliot, and he knew that
there were worse fates than being in prison. Elliot had warned
him on more than one occasion what might happen to him if
he ever turned traitor.

"If you ever think about turning on us, man, I'll get you.
When you least expect it, I'll get you. And the thing is," Elliot
had sneered, "I bet none of your so-called friends will even
notice you're missing."

A. C. knew that Elliot had meant every word, and he shud-
dered. Yes, there were definitely worse things than prison. *So
I guess I better get used to my new home,* A. C. thought to himself as he lay down on his flimsy mattress.

For the first time in weeks, Jenny's parents came to Louisville to see her. It had already been a difficult day emotionally. She'd just gotten home from the hospital. Apprehension about the visit filled her with dread. The moment her parents knocked on the door, the depression she had lived with for so long turned to anger. She refused to look her parents in the eyes when they walked in. She barely responded to their polite greeting and formal embraces.

"You don't look well, Jenny," her mom replied. "Are you doing what the doctors said?"

Jenny nodded.

Her dad cleared his throat and hesitantly spoke, "These are the things in life that cause us to grow so that we won't fall back into the same traps again. I hope you'll never forget what you have put us all through. The entire family, even your grandparents. It's been terrible for us all. I know this has been a tough experience for you, Jenny."

"You have *no* idea what kind of an experience this has been," she said, interrupting the beginning of an almost certain parental lecture.

"We didn't cause this, honey," Jenny's dad said as he looked away.

"But you made sure that it would be hell," Jenny said, with a harshness her parents had never heard before.

Her parents looked at each other and back at her but said nothing.

Finally her father said in a hushed tone, "How dare you talk to me that way." His eyes darted over to Mrs. Elton, "Let's go."

"We just got here," Mrs. Elton said.

"I don't care," Mr. Elton said louder.

"Fine. Go," Jenny shot back. "Why don't both of you just go back to Indy and disown me. That's what you'd really like to do. Isn't it, Daddy?"

"I can't believe this. After all we've been through to pay for your care. You should be grateful," he said, enraged.

"Grateful? Grateful to be shunned? To be sent away like dirty laundry?" Jenny said through tears. "I'm your daughter. I never stopped being your daughter. I'm someone you are supposed to love no matter what. But a few months ago you made a decision that looks to me like you don't want to be my father. So go ahead. Leave!"

"I have done everything for you. I've given one hundred and ten percent to you. And what do YOU do? What do I receive for MY sacrifice? Lies, distrust, and now this. Do you have any shame left? Any shame whatsoever?"

"Dad, I live every moment in shame. But I think sometime we all need to get past that."

"I'll be waiting in the car," Mr. Elton said to Jenny's mom. He grabbed his coat and huffed away.

Jenny couldn't bear to look at her mom.

Her mother looked from the door back to Jenny. She looked helpless and forlorn. "He's not been himself lately. He loves you. You know that."

"He's waiting for you, Mom," Jenny said, turning away from her mother.

The first thing Autumn noticed when she walked into school that morning was the crowd gathered in the lobby. She was afraid a fight had broken out, but her suspicions were quickly dispelled when Melissa ran up to her and grabbed her by the arm as her means of welcome.

"Hey, girl! You just seem to have everything going your way these days! So, did your little senator friend put in a good word for you?" Melissa asked with a wink.

"Melissa, what on earth are you talking about?" Autumn was in no mood to play games this early in the morning.

"Well, duh! The National Speech and Drama Competition team? Hello? Oh, OK, pretend you're surprised, but don't forget the peeps when you get to be famous . . ."

At that point, Autumn had tuned Melissa out. *The results are today! How could I have forgotten?* Making the state team and going to L.A. had been one of Autumn's top goals for this year. But working on Jim Cleary's campaign staff had succeeded in displacing the importance of the team.

As politely as possible, Autumn nudged her way through the crowd to the bulletin board. She knew too well that Melissa's gossip frequently left a lot to be desired in the accuracy department, so she wanted to see the results for herself. This time, however, Melissa apparently had gotten her story straight; there under the "debate" category was Autumn's name.

"I made it! I made it!" someone screamed in Autumn's ear. She spun around to see who was responsible for deafening her. As she did, Zack grabbed her by both hands and started swinging her around. The crowd parted and watched the pair with amusement. Autumn couldn't help but laugh at Zack's contagious excitement. He finally quit spinning her when Jill and Kandi ran up to see what was going on.

"I made the 'drama division,'" Zack sang out, this time grabbing Jill and taking her for a spin. Jill squealed with delight and fell into Zack's arms, laughing.

"And I made the team in debate," added Autumn.

"Well, I probably could have figured that one out," teased Kandi.

"Oh, Zack! I'm so proud of you!" Jill cried, giving him another hug.

"Let's get out of here!" Zack said.

"What?" Autumn asked.

"Let's scram!"

"Well, I kind of have school," Autumn said, stating the obvious.

"You know what you're problem is?" Zack said, smiling.

"Uh, which one?" Autumn asked.

"The omnipresent problem. The I-can't-have-fun-cuz-I'm-supposed-to-be-perfect problem. The I-haven't-missed-school-since-the-Reagan-administration problem. The—"

"I get the point!" Autumn said laughing. "Sorry, Zack. Can't skip school."

Zack shook his head. "We all have our own demons to battle. For some it's insanity. For others, it's depression. For you, it's addiction to the smell of cafeteria mystery meat and athletic socks."

Jill laughed loudly as Zack's Robin Williams tangent continued.

"Autumn! You're growing up too fast. Before long, as Willie Shakespeare so distinctly noted, you'll enter the last stage."

"What?"

"The decrepit second childishness and mere oblivion. Sans teeth, sans eyes, sans taste, sans everything."

Even Autumn laughed at that. "Don't worry, Zack. No gingivitis and perfect vision here."

Zack turned to Jill and got down on one knee. "Therefore, my love?"

Jill covered her mouth a little embarrassed by the crowd of students that now focused on their conversation. "Yes?" Jill finally said.

"She speaks!" Zack said in an Elizabethan manner. "It is my lady. My love! O! That she knew she were."

Zack swooped Jill up and turned to the twenty or so students, "Adieu, adieu, parting is such sweet sorrow." The students applauded as he returned Jill to her feet. He grabbed her hand and they headed for the parking lot.

Kandi said to Autumn, "Can you believe I actually considered dating the guy?"

"He *is* cute," Autumn said, still smiling at his improvisational performance.

"I can't believe you're saying that," Kandi responded as she looked strangely at Autumn.

"I'm not saying I'd even think for a split second about dating him, but he has such a zest for life," Autumn replied. "He's got a great future if he can ever get a grip. He's got an incredible memory. Last week in English he recited the entire first scene of Hamlet. I doubt he'll even get a reprimand for skipping today. Teachers love him and the administration is gaga over him. They think he might be the next Ben Affleck."

Autumn's observations left Kandi flabbergasted. "But that's unfair!"

"Who said life was fair?" Autumn said.

"Gotta go. Check you later. Lunch?" Kandi asked.

"Meet me at my car," Autumn replied.

After school was dismissed, Kandi scanned the mass exit of students for Justin. She knew what to look for: a bright red windbreaker and a lanky companion—Clipper. They finally appeared, five minutes after the bell, talking to Eli. Kandi briskly walked over to the three.

"Hey, guys,"

"The Kandi girl. What are you still doing here?" Clipper said.

"Just looking for Justin," Kandi said.

"Wow, I wish I was being pursued by beautiful women," Clipper said.

Kandi slapped him hard on the shoulder.

"Watch it! That's my shooting arm!" he said, simultaneously chuckling and wincing from the pain.

"Justin, I have a favor to ask," Kandi said.

"Sure. But I've got basketball practice in ten minutes," Justin said, checking the broken wristwatch in his pocket.

"Oh, I completely forgot," Kandi said.

"What do you need? Maybe I can help after practice," Justin offered.

Eli and Clipper started toward the gym, leaving Kandi and Justin alone.

"It's about Zack," Kandi said.

"Don't tell me, you're thinking about dating him again," Justin said.

"Yeah, right . . ." Kandi said sarcastically. "Get real Justin."

"That's a relief. You know how I get," Justin said as he reached for her hand.

"I know this is gonna be weird . . ."

"OK," Justin said seriously.

Kandi exhaled loudly as she tried to put a logical spin on her request. "I just have this weird feeling about Zack. I feel like something's going on. Jill checked back into class this morning and she looked terrible. Very quiet."

"Did you try to talk to her?" Justin asked.

"We don't really have good track record when it comes to meaningful dialogue," Kandi explained. "I don't think I'm the one to talk to her. She's very territorial when it comes to Zack. She practically accused me the other day of trying to destroy their relationship. She thinks I'm still interested."

"In Zack?"

"Right."

Justin paused, trying to understand where Kandi was going with all this. "So what does this have to do with me?" he asked.

"I wanted to see if you'd check on him. I'm concerned."

"Why?" Justin said.

"Maybe Zack and Jill are right. Maybe I'm just being para-noid. I'm just worried about him, especially after the other night at the quarry. He's just so . . . extreme. And he seems to have gotten worse even in the short time I've known him. So I'm thinking that maybe he's mentally off or maybe—like I said, I don't know—maybe, oh, I hate to say it, but I wonder if he's on drugs."

"Why would you think that?"

"His outrageous behavior for starters. I see stuff that reminds me of my dad. I guess it's the happiness that's too extreme to be real."

"So you want me to go over to his house and just show up at his doorstep? Kandi, I'm a little uncomfortable with that. Besides, what would I say? 'Hi, Zack, are you on drugs?'"

"I don't blame you," Kandi said. "I guess I thought if you saw something or had a gut feeling . . . or . . ."

"You know I'd swim the ocean for you."

"I'm not asking you to swim, Justin."

"OK, I'll go," Justin finally said.

As Justin walked to his car after practice, he wondered what excuse he could come up with for going to see Zack. Clipper had hitched a ride with Eli at Justin's request. Justin had tried to explain the situation to Clipper as best he could without revealing Kandi's suspicions. The truth was that in some situations, having Clipper around created more stress than normal, especially in awkward situations. His honesty, many times, proved to be too brutal.

As Justin drove toward Zack's house he looked down at the sticky note where Kandi had jotted down his address. Zack lived in an affluent neighborhood called Clayton's Retreat. The houses were nestled beautifully along the outer realm of an immense golf course. This only added to Justin's discomfort about his pop-in visit. *I've got to work on my ability to say no,* he thought. *Zack is just nuts. Kandi's overreacting.*

After a few wrong turns, Justin finally pulled into Zack's driveway. His heart rate accelerated as he tried to determine what he would say to Zack. *Why did I come?* he rehearsed to himself, scheming for an answer. *To tell the truth, I'm here because Kandi thinks you're more crazy than ever!* Somehow he didn't think he'd use that excuse. Finally he rang the doorbell and prayed that no one would answer. After fifteen seconds, he backed away. "Mission accomplished. Can't say I didn't try," he whispered to himself as he turned to head back to his car.

Just as Justin's hand reached the driver's side door, he heard a woman call out, "Did you ring? I'm sorry I couldn't get off the phone in time to answer the door."

"Yes, ma'am," Justin said.

"Friend of Zack's?" she asked.

"Yes. I just wanted to—"

"Come on in. I'm Zack's mom," she introduced herself.

Justin's jumpy nerves resumed as he quickly forced himself back up the front lawn to the door. "I'm Justin. Sorry I didn't call. This is gonna sound kind of strange, but I just wanted to see how Zack was doing."

"So you know he's sick," she concluded.

"Actually . . . you see, I wasn't sure. I just—"

"He came back home around ten this morning, went straight to his room, and I haven't seen him since," Zack's mom said. "He has his days, you know. Top of the world one moment and then he bottoms out the next."

"Do you mind if I say hi?"

"Course not. He needs somebody to kick him in the pants. Sometimes I wonder about him," she said. "His room is the third door on the left down that hall."

Justin was amazed by the elegance of Zack's home, which was furnished with leather couches and easy chairs, dark green carpet, and a big-screen TV. Justin made his way quietly down the hall, feeling very uncomfortable. He knocked on the door and waited for a response. No answer. He knocked again. Finally the door opened. Zack looked like he had awakened from a long nap and smiled sheepishly when he saw Justin. "Hey. Wasn't exactly expecting to see you."

"Sorry, Zack. I'll go. I didn't mean to wake you," Justin said, backing up into the hallway.

"It's OK. I wasn't sleeping, just resting. I came home after Jill and I left school. I have these headaches every now and then that make me feel like someone chewed my brain up and spit it back onto my neck," Zack said.

"Now that's what I call a visual image," Justin said with a chuckle.

"So what can I do you for?" Zack asked.

"I just wanted to see if you were all right."

Zack looked closer, "Why?"

Justin decided to tell the whole truth. "Actually Kandi asked me to come by and check on you. Please don't tell her that I told you. But it's the only way to explain my sudden appearance," Justin said.

"Kandi?"

"Please don't tell her I told you," Justin repeated.

"Sure. Of course not. I hope you know that she's really a great girl. She loves you. I know she does."

Justin didn't know how to react to Zack's sudden proclamation, so he changed the subject. "So she's gonna want a full report. I think it says a lot about her that she's so concerned about you."

"It says that you're a very lucky guy. She cares for me. She loves you."

With a quick chortle Justin minimized Zack's proclamation. "Would you cut it out. You're beginning to sound like a Back Street Boys lyric."

"You can tell her I'm fine, just got this headache," Zack said.

"Well if you need anything . . ."

"Serious?" Zack asked.

"Sure. Why?" Justin said, thinking, *What would he ever need from me? He seems to have it all. And he's certainly as normal as the rest of us. He probably loves "the show" he puts on, nothing more.* Justin was glad he'd be able to put Kandi's fears to rest.

"This is embarrassing, Justin. I hate this," Zack said slowly.

"What?"

"See, today right after I left school with Jill I noticed that my wallet was gone. Like a stupid idiot I left it in my car with the doors unlocked. I wasn't planning on staying at school. I planned to be gone only a minute while I checked to see if I made it into the drama competition. I knew if I made it, I'd be too excited to sit through class and if I didn't, I'd be a blubbering idiot. And who wants to be around someone like that? So I just, you know, left it in the car. And when I get back in there, no wallet. I can't find it anywhere."

"Did you tell your mom or—"

"That would be suicide. I've already lost my wallet twice, and I can't bear to tell them that I did it again. They get rabid about this kind of stuff. They'd knock me out of the area code."

"I understand," Justin said.

"Anyway, I'm getting some money Friday, but I have this fifty-dollar problem," Zack said and then paused.

Justin stood there trying to comprehend the situation. *Here I am in a castle and the guy's asking me for a loan. This is weird,* he thought.

"I never do this. I swear I don't. But I wondered if maybe you could just lend me fifty until Friday. I promise, Friday and it's back in your wallet," Zack said.

"I don't have that kind of cash on me," Justin said.

Zack lowered his head. "I understand."

Justin paused as he measured the situation carefully. "But why don't I just write you a check?" he offered.

"You will? Man! Thanks!" Zack said.

Justin smiled as he walked over to Zack's desk to use a pen. Justin noticed out of the corner of his eye that Zack's hand had a slight tremor.

"I've definitely been fritzed about it. Look, I'm sorry to even ask you."

"If you can get it back to me by Friday, I'm cool. I won't even miss it. But I do need the money back Friday," Justin said.

"No problem at all. I don't know what to say. Thanks."

10

That night, Autumn and Kandi waited outside the Market Square Arena for Justin and Clipper. They had gotten tickets to the annual Christian Rock Jam, featuring D.C. Talk, Sonic Flood, and the News Boys.

"This is such a pain. The show starts in ten minutes. Why couldn't we have just all gone together?" Autumn asked.

"Basketball," Kandi replied.

"Already? It's not even October!" Autumn asked in a bewildered voice.

"Get used to it. Guys are hopeless if they aren't chasing, kicking, swatting, or dunking some kind of spherical object," Kandi said.

"Good one!" Autumn said, laughing.

Finally Justin appeared behind them. "Hey, girls. Waiting for someone?" he asked, his hair still wet from the quick post-practice shower. "Look who else is here."

From behind Justin, Eli came into view. His presence surprised Autumn. "I thought you weren't coming."

"Didn't think I could. Then Clipper backed out and gave me his ticket," Eli said.

"Really? He backed out? He's the one who orchestrated this whole night," Autumn said in shock.

"Don't act so disappointed," Eli said.

"I'm not, Eli. Just surprised," Autumn quickly responded.

"Clipper's having a tough time. Emotionally, I mean," Justin said.

"Jenny?" Kandi asked.

"Jenny and about two hundred other things," Justin replied. "The fact that the police questioned him about the bomb really shook him up. I'm pretty sure they know Clipper wasn't involved. But I guess he kind of feels like God's just broken a lot of promises. He's not exactly on fire spiritually right now," Justin said.

"That's hard for me to imagine," Kandi said.

"He's always been so strong," Autumn added.

At the first opportunity, Kandi pulled Justin aside. "So how did your visit with Zack go?"

"OK, I guess."

"How did he look? What did he say? Did he seem freaked out or anything?" asked anxiously.

"Basically, he looked terrible but he seemed to be OK."

"Did you think he'd been drinking?" Kandi said quietly just a few inches from his ear.

"No. He didn't smell like it. He didn't look or act strung out either. But he was shaky. I think that was because he said he had a bad headache."

"That's weird. Don't you think that's weird? He seemed like he was feeling great that morning," Kandi said.

"I don't know, Kandi. My aunt gets horrible migraines and they come out of nowhere. Zack looked like she does when she gets one."

"What else did he say?"

Justin reached his threshold of questions and shrugged his shoulders. "Kandi, what more can I tell you? He lives in a posh neighborhood, has a nice mom, and said he had a killer headache. He didn't smell or act drunk. He was very shaky. That's it." Justin paused and then threw in, "And he asked me for a loan."

"A loan?"

"Yes."

"Money?"

"Kandi! Of course," Justin said.

"What did you do?" Kandi asked.

"I wrote him a check. He said he lost his wallet or maybe somebody stole it. He said he didn't want to ask his mom, so I loaned him fifty."

"You loaned Zack fifty dollars?" Kandi said, surprised.

"Kandi, you are acting like that's the dumbest thing I could have done. I went over there because you asked me. Don't tell me you're shocked that I loaned him money."

"Aren't you afraid you won't ever see that money again?" Kandi asked.

"No. They're filthy rich. You know that. He said he just needed the money until Friday," Justin said defensively.

Justin stewed during the entire concert, angry that he did

exactly what she wanted him to do and now she had morphed into this hand-wringing mother figure.

After the concert the four friends decided to split up; Autumn would drop off Eli at his house and Justin would take Kandi back to her apartment. Kandi sensed Justin's anger and tried to get him talking.

"I'm sorry I upset you, Justin," Kandi said softly.

"I'm not upset," Justin said in monotone.

"Fine," Kandi said with her own dose of resentment.

"OK, maybe I am a little perturbed. It's just that sometimes I don't understand where you're coming from," Justin stated.

"I'm just worried about him. I'm afraid he's out of control, and I was just skeptical that throwing money his direction is really helping."

"Maybe you're right, but this is the deal. I thought you'd be grateful that I would have the heart to loan him the money and instead I feel like you just wagged your finger in my face," Justin admitted honestly.

"I'm sorry. I was wrong," Kandi said. "You're right."

"Don't worry, Kandi. I won't tell anybody."

Kandi's heart warmed. She felt a closeness to Justin that she hadn't felt in a long time. *He could have just lied about his feelings, but as uncomfortable as it was to him, he told the truth. He let me know,* she thought. Honest communication was unheard of in her home where an alcoholic father had made deception a way of life. She moved over to the center of the front seat and rested her head on Justin's shoulder as he drove her home.

Friday afternoon, Justin had nearly worked himself into a rage. He was sure Zack avoided him at school. He only saw him once, and he was sure they'd made eye contact, but Zack walked away before Justin could even talk to him. *Zack's not going to repay the loan,* he thought to himself. *How could I have been so gullible?* When he got home, he went straight to his room, ignoring everyone in the house.

Justin couldn't imagine asking anyone for a loan. That, to him, was unthinkable. His weakness had always been an over-reliance on himself. But even if he had asked for a loan he would rather have fallen over dead than face the humiliation of hiding from the lender because he couldn't repay the money.

Justin grabbed the phone to call Kandi. He hated this part more that anything. Now he had to call his date and tell her that he didn't have the change to take her out because he loaned his money to the guy she went out with a couple of weeks ago. It just sounded too much like a Jerry Springer show.

Kandi answered the phone.

"I'm sorry, Kandi," Justin said dryly without even saying hello.

"OK."

"You were right. You told me I shouldn't have done it and—"

"He didn't pay you back," Kandi said finishing his sentence.

"I can't believe the nerve of the guy!" Justin exclaimed.

"It's really my fault. I'm the one who sent you over there on the investigative assignment," Kandi said.

"I must admit that if I hadn't wanted to impress you so much by showing how giving I was, I never would have done that. You wield great power," Justin said with a smile.

"I know you too well. You're a tightwad," Kandi said.

"But I tried," Justin answered.

"I know."

Just then Justin's doorbell rang. "Kandi, can I call you right back? Somebody's at the door."

"Sure. Now you can tell whoever that is that you gave at the office and halfway mean it."

"Real funny."

"Bye."

Justin ambled wearily to the door and opened it.

"Zack! Man, am I surprised to see you."

"Why? I owe you money, don't I? Sorry I didn't get this to you today. Really embarrassing. I left it at home. I hated to leave you hanging like that."

"No problem," Justin said.

"Bet you and Kandi will find something to do with it. You know, I have to tell you something. I know you're a Christian. Kandi told me about all that. I never gave Christianity a second thought. That's kind of why I asked you for a loan. I wanted to see if Christians really are different. And I guess it's true," Zack said.

Justin just stared back not knowing what to say. Zack's speech blew him away. *Is that really the reason why he asked for money. Is he really testing the waters?* Justin wondered. "Well, thanks. Glad I passed the test."

"Me too. By the way. They found my wallet at school. Can you believe it? I mean, I got my paycheck today anyway, but wow! Today's been lots better. Gotta run."

"Thanks, Zack. Let me know if I can ever help in the future."

"Thanks. I hope I don't have to, but you never know, do ya?"

Justin shook his head.

Zack turned back around as he walked toward this car. "Hope I can return the favor sometime."

As Justin went back to his room, he felt guilty for judging Zack so quickly. He couldn't believe the conversation and the fact that Zack seemed wide open to faith. He went back to his room and pressed the redial button. Kandi answered immediately. "So who was it? Avon lady calling?"

"You won't believe it," Justin said

"Zack?" Kandi guessed.

"Yeah. He came to pay back the money he borrowed."

"That's a relief," Kandi said. "How'd he look? Still on the fritz?"

"He looked great, Kandi. Really . . . peaceful. In fact, he seemed better than I've ever seen him," Justin said.

"Maybe I judged him too quickly," Kandi said, feeling some regret over the conversation she'd had with Jill.

"That's not the half of it. You know what he told me? He said that part of the reason he asked me for the loan was so that he could see if my Christianity was real."

"Get out!" Kandi nearly shouted into the receiver.

"Really," Justin said.

"I guess I've been way off base. I practically branded him as a junkie," Kandi said.

"He's really searching. I just happened to peel off a little of the mask," Justin said.

The following Saturday Autumn arose early to leave for the Indiana Meeting for the National Speech and Dramatic Arts Competition, which was held in Columbus, Indiana. She, Zack, and another student were carpooling to the meeting. Autumn had hesitated going with the group, especially when Zack offered to drive. She couldn't forget the conversations that she'd had with Kandi about his reckless lifestyle.

But still, it was only a forty-five-minute drive. Autumn was afraid she would seem like a snob if she chose to drive there by herself. She knew she already appeared that way to many students who didn't even know her. She regretted that many thought of her as a one-dimensional person only interested in achievements and grades. She spent many nights searching herself, taking inventory of her lifestyle, looking for whether that portrait was true.

She drove to the school where they planned to meet. As usual, she arrived early and wrote in her prayer journal while she waited for the others.

God, I pray that You'll help me give Zack a fair chance. Open my eyes to who he really is. After so many days of critically picking his behavior apart, looking for chinks in his armor, I'm afraid I've sought more to prove that he's on the verge of catastrophe and less trying to really be his friend.

After a few minutes the other student, Ann Hamilton, pulled into the school parking lot. About the same time, Zack drove up in his Jeep, wearing black jeans, sandals, a Pearl Jam T-shirt, and dark sunglasses.

"Let's rock," he said over the blaring of the stereo.

Autumn felt a dull ache in the pit of her stomach. *I hope I'm not making a huge mistake,* she thought to herself. "Hey, why don't we just go in my car," she proposed. "More room," she offered with an innocent grin.

Zack got out of his car and walked over to Autumn's Taurus. He peered into the dash. "What kind of sound system you got in there?" he asked, smiling.

Autumn shrugged her shoulders, "I don't know. Came with the car."

"Nah. Not up to specs," Zack said, dismissing her offer.

"Don't be a stick-in-the-mud," Ann said to Autumn. Ann knew Zack well since she was also a member of the drama program. It also seemed to Autumn, by the way she immediately called her a stick-in-the-mud, that Ann knew Autumn by reputation. *Am I really being a stick-in-the-mud? It's just a short drive. Loosen up!* she silently scolded herself.

"OK, no problem," Autumn said, trying to be as laid-back about the trip as possible. "Just throwing out the option."

They hopped into the Jeep and started their journey to Columbus. Although Columbus was normally a forty-five-minute drive, Autumn realized that they'd arrive much sooner. Zack scorched the interstate, setting the cruise at ninety miles an hour.

"Is this your normal speed?" Autumn asked, trying not to sound too motherly.

"No," Zack said.

"Well, you really don't have to rush; we have plenty of time," Autumn said, gesturing toward the clock in the dashboard.

"I think you misunderstood me. This is definitely not my normal speed. I'm driving a little slower so that you don't have a heart attack," Zack said, smiling into the rearview mirror.

Without warning, Zack exited the interstate and pulled into a McDonalds. "I've got a serious case of the munchies. How 'bout you guys?"

"Sure," Ann said.

"Fine with me," Autumn replied.

Autumn hated McDonalds. She ordered a Diet Coke and waited for her two companions. Ann and Zack joined her with a tray full of grub.

"I tell you, Zack," Ann began. "Jill is absolutely goo-goo-eyed in love with you."

Zack looked away. Autumn couldn't believe it. Could the guy actually be embarrassed?

"Got her fooled, don't I?" he said.

"I think she's lucky to have a guy like you," Ann said, eyes fixed solely on him.

"So what's she like?" Autumn asked, rescuing Zack from an uncomfortable moment.

"She's really a nice girl. Too nice for me," Zack said.

"What do you mean?" Autumn asked.

"We all have our little problems, don't we?" Zack replied.

"I guess. But like what?" Autumn asked hesitantly.

"So are you like some kind of shrink?" Zack said defensively.

"Sorry," Autumn said realizing she did sound a little like an interrogator.

Ann spoke next. "I'll tell you my problems if you tell me yours," she said, suddenly challenging the other two to an impromptu game of truth-telling.

"Sounds fun," Zack said. "Go ahead."

"When I was about six years old, my parents got a divorce. It turned out to be a really ideal divorce if there is such a thing. They just walked into the living room one day and said, 'Kids, we are so sorry to tell you, but you need to know this. Sorry we didn't tell you earlier, but we're splitting up.' I barely knew what it meant. But my brother and I found out pretty quickly.

"It was really OK for us," Ann continued. "We saw dad every weekend, and everyone seemed to be doing fine. But then when I turned thirteen, my dad came to my birthday party and my parents got in this big argument. Dad brought this guy to the party, and I thought he was just an old friend or something. My parents didn't think I could hear them. They screamed in whispers. It's strange how people do that. So I heard just fine. Turns out my dad's gay. Some joke, huh? On my thirteenth birthday, of all days. Steve, my brother, found out too. I told him. That was a mistake. It made him crazy. From then until he turned nineteen he was riding this roller coaster. He tried to kill himself twice."

Silence blanketed the table. Autumn swallowed hard, searching for a response. Finally Zack spoke, "Want to hear mine?"

"Sure," Autumn said. Ann nodded.

Zack leaned in toward the girls on the other side of the table, "I'm me. And believe me, that's enough."

Ann laughed loudly. Autumn looked at Zack strangely.

"Now that's a cop-out," Autumn said seriously. "Ann just bared her soul and you give us the evil eye and say 'I'm me'?"

"Give me a break, Autumn. The only reason you're not laughing is that you wanted to find out some dainty morsels about my demons so you can have some reason to judge me," Zack said, calmly eating his burger.

The comment really hurt Autumn. "That's not true," she protested.

"No?" Zack probed.

"Absolutely not," Autumn replied.

"What's your story?" Zack said, turning the spotlight on Autumn.

"I don't really have—"

"Everyone has a story," Zack said, interrupting Autumn's stammer.

"I guess my story is that I'm black. Add to that I'm a preacher's kid, and I happen to be a square peg constantly rubbing against a round hole. Everybody can find some reason to discount me," Autumn said, looking away from them. Her eyes moistened. "Everybody can find something to say behind my

back. I move into your neighborhood, and I know there's at least
one old school Anglo who'll grumble about me. He'll use the 'n'
word around his friends. And then there's the people who could
care less that I'm black. They just have a chip on their shoulder
that I'm at the top of my class or that I'm a virgin, or that I don't
drink, or that my dad's a preacher. When it comes to criticism,
there's plenty of me to go around," Autumn ended vehemently.

"I'm sorry," Zack said. "I just—"

"No, I'm sorry. I didn't mean to unload like that," Autumn
said.

"But it felt kind of good, didn't it? You ought to do it more
often," Zack said. "I do it all the time. I'm like a human gum-
ball machine. Stick a quarter in and whatever I'm thinking just
rolls straight from my noodle to the tip of my tongue in less
than three seconds. Guess that's my Achilles' heel."

Autumn sat there and drank her soda in silence. She wasn't
accustomed to being around someone who was so totally
uninhibited, and she wasn't sure she liked it. *Maybe that's it.
His lack of inhibition and his complete command of truthfulness is intimidating,* she thought to herself.

After they finished eating, the three returned to the Jeep.
Autumn trailed right behind Zack as he reached for his keys in
his front jean pocket. As he pulled them out a small, square
packet no larger than a postage stamp fell out of his pocket and
onto the blacktop. Autumn looked closer and saw that it held
a white powdery substance. Her back stiffened. Her suspicions
immediately and powerfully returned.

"Zack? You dropped something," Autumn said cooly, wondering how he'd react.

Zack turned around and quickly picked it up, returning it to his pocket. They drove for ten minutes without another word. Finally Zack broke the silence. "Autumn," he said casually, "I can imagine what you must be thinking." Zack shook his head and chuckled, still looking straight ahead at the road. "Know what that stuff is that fell out of my pocket?"

Autumn's mind raced. She thought for a moment and then said, "No, but I know your specialty is telling the truth," she said, joking through her anxiety.

"It may be hard for you to accept," Zack said.

"Try me," Autumn replied, her mind swirling with curiosity.

"It's headache powder," Zack said.

"It's what?" she had to hear him say it again.

"Headache powder," Zack repeated.

Ann threw her head back and laughed hysterically. "You're kidding! Headache powder, as in Goody's?"

Autumn clenched her teeth. She didn't believe a word of it.

"Yes. You do know about migraines, don't you?" Zack said amused at Ann. "That's the only thing that seems to work."

"I feel like we've stepped into a commercial," Ann said, still laughing.

"Laugh all you want. Just wait till you get kicked in the tail by one, and you'll come crawling to me for help. But don't snort it. Just throw your head back and knock it down with a Coke," Zack said. "Now that's Coke as in soft drink, not as in the stuff you thought I had," Zack said, turning his head to glance back at Autumn. Ann laughed again.

Autumn dropped the subject and tried to forget the odd conversation, but she couldn't. *Why would he carry headache powder in a small plastic pack?* The more she thought about it the more absurd the entire story became. *There were some things that would cause Zack's truthfulness to falter,* Autumn concluded.

Autumn picked up the phone and returned it to its cradle ten times that night after she returned from Columbus. She felt she had to talk to Jill. Zack's personality had changed drastically after the meeting. During the meeting he stole the show. He had the charisma and quick humor of a professional improvisational comedian, but he cratered on the way home. He drove with a vengeance, quickly braking when his radar detector sounded. Even Ann became worried about him. It seemed that he couldn't keep the act up for a long stretch. He was very intent on getting home.

Autumn finally dialed the number and wait for an answer.

"Hello?"

"Hey, Jill? This is Autumn."

"Oh, hi! When did you guys get back?" Jill asked.

"We got back about an hour ago," Autumn said.

"Oh."

Jill's disappointment was obvious to Autumn. "So he hasn't called yet?"

"No," Jill answered. "I'm sure he'll call later. He's a night owl. Did you have fun? Zack's a trip, isn't he?"

"He's definitely that and more," Autumn replied.

After a moment or so of awkward silence, Autumn went on to explain why she had called.

"Look, Jill, I really hesitated to call you about this, but—"

"What is it?" Jill asked, suddenly in a panic. "Did something happen? Is Zack all right?"

"I'm trying to tell you, Jill. This isn't easy for me," Autumn said.

"Will you stop this. You're freaking me out."

"I'm just worried about, Zack. I'm concerned that he has a drug problem. I tried to confront him and he just denies it," Autumn finally said.

"Oh, why?" Jill asked, suddenly calm.

"I saw something, and I asked him about it. He said there was no problem whatsoever, but I can't—"

"You think he'd lie to you?" Jill interrupted.

"I don't know . . . it just seems improbable that he'd be carrying around some white powdery substance in his pocket that wasn't some kind of drug," Autumn said and waited for a reaction.

Jill sat in stony silence.

"OK, so there you have it," Autumn said. "What are you thinking? Talk to me."

"I think you've got a lot of nerve making that kind of a claim," Jill nearly spat into the phone.

"I'm just worried that he might have a real problem," Autumn said.

"I know him. I love him. Zack is a special guy."

"I agree," Autumn inserted.

"Nobody understands him. You think, 'Wow he's a creative genius. He must be on coke—'"

"I didn't say that," Autumn said defensively.

"You might as well have," Jill shouted back.

"I'm just concerned—"

"Then keep your concerns to yourself, OK?" Jill hissed.

"Why are you making me the enemy?" Autumn said.

Click. Jill hung up on her.

Clipper dragged himself out of bed and forced himself into the kitchen to make an appearance. He slid into a chair and stared bleakly at the steaming breakfast in front of him.

"Hey, Clip. Do you think you'll be ready for church on time?" his dad asked.

"I'm not going," Clipper stated.

"Don't you think it would do you some good? You skipped youth group once this week. Shawn's going to wonder what's up," Clipper's dad said.

"I doubt it," Clipper replied.

"You're being too hard on yourself," Mr. Hayes said as he got up from the table.

"Dad, please, I just don't feel good. I don't feel like going to church today," Clipper said as he took a tentative bite of eggs.

"All right, fine. Honey? You ready?"

Mrs. Hayes walked into the kitchen and kissed Clipper on the cheek before she and Mr. Hayes walked out. *Why do I feel like I'm living on the set of* Leave It to Beaver? Clipper wondered to himself after they left.

He sat for a while, thinking about his life. The longer he sat there in the silence, the darker his despair grew. He finally laid down on the couch and stared at the ceiling as the tears rolled down into his ears.

"God, are You there? 'Cause I don't know anymore. I don't know if You even care. Can't You see how I've tried to do everything I thought You wanted me to do? I always thought You had a plan. I thought following You was a formula. I do this and You do that. I pray; You answer. But I just don't know anymore. Oh, God," Clipper said sobbing. "I prayed for Jenny to come home and it didn't happen. I prayed for A. C. and he's in jail. I thought if I stepped out—if I stepped out in faith, if I gave You everything—gave it all to you, that You'd open his heart. But now I don't know anything anymore. I only know I don't want to lose my faith in You."

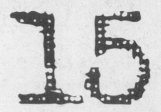

At 8:30 Monday morning A. C. walked into the conference room of the Juvenile Detention Facility. The meeting was at his request. His attorney had arranged the meeting with Detective Fuller after A. C. made his decision. He decided to come clean regardless of the consequences.

"We'll be taping this, A. C." Detective Fuller said.

"Fine," A. C. said in a low voice.

"It's your time. You want to talk. I'm listening." The detective sat back, his expression expectant.

"Have you found Elliot?"

"No," Fuller said. "That's not your concern right now, though. You tell me *your* story."

"I met Elliot at a party last spring and started hanging around with him and some of his friends. It was all fun and games for me. He was into everything—alcohol, drugs, prostitutes—everything imaginable. And anything anyone wanted, he could provide. He had this inner circle of guys he called The Association. They were the elite. They had secret meetings. They had a brotherhood. They were a kind of family. And since I didn't have any, it appealed to me. A place to belong, you know?"

Detective Fuller nodded but said nothing.

"Elliot energized this elite group with his own anger at churches and society. I understood his hatred because I felt the same way."

"Why?" Fuller asked.

A. C. shrugged. "I guess I was angry that I didn't have what everyone else seemed to have. Those people despised me, so I despised them because they judged me without knowing me. They turned away and treated me like dirt. And churches are always saying how awful people like me are."

"What did Elliot want for his group?"

"He wanted power. He wanted to do something big so people would be afraid of him, so he could show them who had the real power. He always wanted to bomb something. He thought that was the best way to scare people. I didn't really know anything about bombs, but I lied and said I could make one. His eyes lit up and all of a sudden, I felt important. It was hard to impress Elliot. But I'd done it. After that, I knew I had to learn all about bombs, so I did.

"Then it became an obsession. I spent hours searching the Internet and reading books until I knew how to do it. When I was ready, Elliot took us all into the country. We experimented there. It was pretty awesome thinking of the destruction we could make, the panic we could send through people.

"About the same time Elliot told The Association about his plan to bomb a school, Clipper started bugging me."

"Clifford Hayes? Is he in the group?" Fuller asked.

"No," A. C. said. "He's this squeaky-clean kid who somehow decided that he had to talk to me about God. He kept showing up at the worst times. So I thought I could scare him away. I threatened him and tried to persuade him, but he just kept coming back."

Fuller made a note on his legal pad. He looked up. "Keep talking about the plan to bomb the school."

"Elliot wanted to bomb a school. He hated his school and thought it would be cool to do away with some of the administrators and geeky kids who hang out in the office kissing up to everyone. I thought it was a bit drastic, but didn't say anything. And this Clipper guy kept at it. And the things he said . . . I don't know, really, what it was. But because he kept at me, I tried to get Elliot to change his mind and bomb an empty church instead. I figured that would still give us a thrill and not hurt anyone."

Detective Fuller stopped taking notes and looked up. "When did you decide to back out?"

"About a week before. I don't know, Detective. It's weird. I've started caring about stuff. And I almost feel embarrassed by the change. I don't understand it. But I just decided that I didn't want to be a part of destruction any more. So I decided to diffuse the bomb."

A. C. glanced at his manacled hands in his lap. "Look, I know I helped build bombs, and you can jail me if you want. But I'm not guilty of planting that bomb. I am guilty of breaking down the door to the church, but that was to cut the wires. I honestly tried to stop The Association. I know you probably won't believe me, but I'm not guilty of anything else."

"OK. So tell me everything that happened that day."

A. C. told him about the early-morning drive he took to the old storm shelter outside of town and how he found The Association's record book with the strange message—Book 3, New Testament. He explained how he broke open the door and searched through the darkness for the bomb and then disarmed it.

Fuller wrote fast and furiously in his notebook, then took a moment to go over his notes. "We found lots of notes on Clifford Hayes' hard drive from a guy who used the nickname van Gogh? Who is he?"

"Elliot," A. C. said.

"Where is Elliot?" Fuller asked.

"I don't know. He may be as far away as Mexico by now, but my guess is he's still here in town," A. C. speculated.

"Why?" A. C.'s lawyer asked.

"Because I'm still alive."

"A white plastic packet, huh?" Justin said to Autumn. "I don't think it was Sweet 'n Low."

"He said it was for a headache," Autumn said.

"It doesn't make sense," Justin added.

"I told Jill—"

"And she said you were off your rocker," Justin said, completing her sentence.

"Basically. I think someone needs to talk to him, but it's not me. I'm sure Jill told Zack that I talked to her. I saw him a few minutes ago, and he practically turned and walked the other way just to avoid me," Autumn said.

"Yep. She told him," Justin concluded, "I'll see what I can do."

Justin didn't see Zack for the rest of the day. He even sacrificed a tardy just to make a quick sprint to the Fine Arts Building where Zack took acting during last period. Mrs. Martinez, the director, said that he had checked out early again. After school he went to Zack's house and rang the doorbell. Mrs. Galloway came to the door and opened it with hesitation.

"Hi. Can I see Zack for a second?"

"Actually, no. He's been grounded," she said tersely.

"Oh . . . OK," Justin said. He tried to think of a way to assess the situation without appearing nosey. He wanted to tell her about what Autumn had seen and their concern about Zack's erratic personality. *But if anyone would be clued in to his personality and would have some hint of drug use it would be her, wouldn't it?* Justin thought. *Perhaps that's the very reason why she grounded him.*

Finally Justin said, "Is there anything I can do?"

Mrs. Galloway looked at him strangely and shook her head.

Justin left the house and drove to the convenience store a few miles away. He pulled up to the pay phone and got out. After analyzing the situation, he decided to call Jill, but he had no idea where she lived. So he looked up the number of someone he never dreamed he would call.

"This is who?" Melissa said flabbergasted.

"Come on, Melissa. You know. Justin," he replied.

"Hold on a sec. Let me barf from shock! I didn't even know you could work a phone," Melissa said laughing.

"Funny," Justin said, without trying to match wits.

"So what do you need?" Melissa asked.

"Do you know Jill Welch?"

"Sure," Melissa replied.

"Where does she live?" Justin asked.

"This is weird. You want to know where Jill Welch lives? Let me get the whole picture here. Kandi dates you. Then she dates Zack. Kandi decides to cool it with him and he dates Jill. Now you want Jill. What's wrong with this picture!?"

"I didn't say I wanted Jill," Justin replied defensively. "I just need to know where she lives. I need to talk to her."

"Why?" Melissa asked.

Justin thought about lying. Perhaps if he said that he needed clarification on a homework assignment or something that would squelch her curiosity. *Why do I even worry?* he finally concluded. "I just need to talk to her about something," he eventually explained.

"Whatever," Melissa replied. "Hold on a sec."

After half a minute she returned. "Her phone number is—"

"I need her address," Justin said.

"Fine. Fine. You don't have to be so curt. Just thought I'd save you some gas money. Her address is 4841 Milton Circle," Melissa said.

"Thanks, Melissa," Justin said.

"Sure. I enjoyed our little visit. Call back when you aren't so pushy," Melissa added.

"I'm sorry. I've gotta go."

Justin got back in his car and headed to Hampton Woods and Milton Circle, wondering what outlandish story Melissa would make of their phone conversation.

Justin brought his old white Caprice to a halt in front of Jill's house, walked to the front door, and rang the bell. When Jill opened the door, he knew that something terrible had happened. She didn't speak or look at him, she only stared down at the ground.

"What's with Zack?" Justin asked.

Jill didn't speak.

"I'm not going to judge you or him," Justin said quietly. "I'm concerned. What is it, Jill?"

"Come in," she said and led him into the living room. After settling into the cushions of the couch, she continued, "I really thought he could handle it all."

"Handle what?"

"Kandi and Autumn were right. I'm so stupid. I tried to cover for him because I loved him and I didn't want him to be in trouble. I do love him. I still do," she said as her chin quivered.

"I went by his house, and his mom said he's grounded. What happened? I want to help," Justin said.

"He's messed up. I didn't know it when we first dated. He's such a charmer. He's so talented and full of life. I caught him taking some pills one afternoon. He said it was just some prescription. But after a while he couldn't hide it from me. He just said that he enjoyed it and that he wasn't addicted to anything. And I believed him. Last night we were over here and everything was great. My parents fell in love with him too. Mom and

Dad even went out to dinner and left us here at the house. They really trusted him, and I did too," Jill said as she buried her head in her hands. Her shoulders trembled as she wept.

"Go on," Justin said softly.

Jill wiped her eyes and took a deep breath. "We watched a movie, and I fell asleep on the couch," she said. "This morning my mom couldn't find the tennis bracelet my dad gave her for their twentieth wedding anniversary. We just assumed it had been misplaced. And then my dad called me at school and said that he was missing three checks from a box he keeps in his office. He called the bank and they said that the records show one of those checks went through at noon for five hundred dollars."

Justin didn't know what to say. He couldn't have imagined the depth of Zack's problem. "Have you talked to Zack since?" Justin asked.

"He called me a few minutes ago and apologized. He said he'd pay everything back. Funny thing is, I still care for him," Jill confessed.

Kandi felt she needed to call Zack after she heard the news from Justin. After pleading with Zack's mother, she was finally allowed to talk to him.

"Zack?"

"Hey, girl. Glad you called. I was about to go nuts here in solitary. Some mess I've gotten myself into, huh?"

"What are you going to do?" Kandi asked.

"I'm going to get down on my hands and knees and ask for mercy. What else can I do? I admit, that was one of the stupidest things I've ever done. It takes the cake. I know I'm going to have to pay the price. I'm going to pay them back. I just got in a bind and started thinking irrationally."

"Drugs have a way of doing that to people," Kandi said quietly.

Zack's silence on the other end of the line scared Kandi.

Finally he said in a stern tone. "Kandi, it doesn't have anything to do with drugs. Don't lay that on me. I've been through enough already."

"Zack, I know where you are. I've told you about all the things my dad went—"

"Give me a BREAK!" Zack yelled. "I'm not your father. I'm not some scum who uses people for a fifth of scotch."

The verbal missile hit Kandi hard. She gasped in shock.

"I'm sorry," Zack said, backing off. "I'm just mixed up right now. I'm going to prove who I really am. I really am sorry. I didn't mean what I said—"

Kandi hung up the phone and wept.

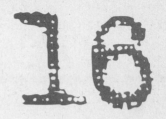

The light poured into A. C.'s cell the next morning. He had tried all night to get warm in the cold cell. His back ached from the cold. For some reason the correction officers at the detention center liked to keep the place cold, and there was nothing A. C. could do about it. For more than a week he had been locked in the same cell, which consisted of a gray concrete bed with a half-inch mattress, a pillow, a sink, a stainless steel toilet, and a roll of toilet paper. He had been monitored constantly by a video camera mounted high above him. He would have liked nothing more than to rip it apart.

"Hey, A. C., get up and come with me," the officer said.

"Why? What's going on?" A. C. asked.

The officer didn't respond. A. C. followed him to the security station, which was a desk elevated two feet above the waxed tile floor. The officer opened a cabinet above the desk

and pulled out a bag that contained the clothes A. C. was
wearing when he was arrested. He dumped the belongings on
the dark cherry wood desk. "Son, I need you to look through
these items and sign here if you agree this is everything you
had on you when you were brought here."

"What's going on?" A. C. said in disbelief. "Am I leaving?"

"You're free to go," the drone-like officer replied. "Your
grandma is out there, along with the lawyer and Detective
Fuller."

A. C. quickly changed clothes after he had signed the prop-
erties document. He walked out to the front lobby, still in
shock that it all happened so suddenly. His grandmother tear-
fully embraced him, but A. C. refused to show any emotion. He
looked at Detective Fuller and said, "What's this all about? Why
are you releasing me?"

"We can't keep you here, son. All the evidence lines up
with your testimony. We're looking for Elliot now. You're on
probation, and you'll have to meet with a parole officer every
other week for the next six weeks. And then every three
months after that for a year," the detective continued.

"And Elliot?"

"We've got APBs all over the country on him. His big mistake was the call he made to you at the jail a couple of nights
ago. Stupid. Must have been drunk or high or something. I
couldn't believe he was that dumb. We tape all the calls that
come into this place so we heard it all—the threats, the missing
pieces to the puzzle. I mean he totally cleared you. It was quite
a breakthrough for you, and I bet you didn't even think about
it," Fuller said.

A. C. shook his head, remembering the call vividly. "So what do I do? He's coming after me."

"Can't stay here," Fuller said as he shrugged his shoulders.

A. C. was scared, but more than anything he wanted out of this place. He grabbed his stuff and left with his grandmother.

Two blocks away a blue Camaro pulled out of its parking place and slowly headed in the same direction.

"You won't believe this, Autumn. They let him go!" Clipper exclaimed over the phone.

"I thought he was being detained without bail," Autumn said in disbelief.

"I know. They cleared him. I called the detention center, and they said he'd been released," Clipper explained.

"Where is he now?" Autumn said.

"I don't know. I guess his grandmother's house. I'm about to call over there. I need to see him," Clipper said.

"If he's there, pick me up on the way. I want to go too," Autumn said.

Clipper called. A. C.'s grandmother answered and said that A. C. had just gotten home and was taking a shower. She surprised Clipper at the end of the short conversation. "Clipper, I don't know you that well, but I know you cared enough to reach out to my grandson. It made a difference."

"I want to come by," Clipper said anxiously.

"We'll be here."

Clipper picked up Autumn and headed for A. C.'s.

"I'm nervous. I don't know what he'll say when he sees me. I was pretty harsh when he first was jailed. But I have to let him know that I prayed for him. I've got some major apologizing to do to God. I've really doubted Him. I felt like He'd forgotten about me," Clipper said.

Two blocks before they reached the house Clipper applied the brakes. "What is it?" Autumn asked, perplexed by his sudden decision to pull over.

"I've seen that car before," he said.

"What?" Autumn looked up and spotted the vehicle.

"I've seen that car before," Clipper repeated. "Look, there's A. C."

A. C. looked over his shoulder at three young men. He began to run. Clipper hit the gas and sped toward them. The three men grabbed A. C. and shoved him into the idling Camaro.

"Autumn! That must be the guys behind the bombing! I've got to follow them. You check on his grandmother and call the police!" Clipper ordered Autumn, pulling over to the curb in front of A. C.'s house to let her out. As he began to pull away in pursuit of the car he saw A. C.'s grandmother stumbling onto the front porch, bleeding from her forehead. Autumn quickly ran to support the old woman and motioned for Clipper to go ahead.

Once inside the house Autumn dialed 9-1-1. "I need to report a kidnapping on West 22nd Avenue. A blue Camaro. I have a friend who is trying to follow them." Her voice was breathless with fear.

The communications officer asked her to hold and when she came back on the line, she said, "We are aware of the situation. One of our officers was keeping an eye on the scene and he's in pursuit. If you have any way to contact your friend, tell him to stay back. The people in that car have guns."

Clipper hit the gas hard and sped down the road. As soon as Elliot's car came into view, Clipper heard the screech of tires as Elliot ran through a stoplight, turning left onto the highway. "They definitely know I'm here," Clipper said to himself as he followed them.

The blue Camaro sped down Merton Road until they came to another stoplight. They turned left and then to Clipper's surprise turned into an unfinished industrial complex. There's no outlet, Clipper thought, perplexed by the move. Deserted bulldozers and construction equipment cluttered the unearthed field. Elliot pulled his car over to the side of the road and came to a stop. Clipper suddenly realized the danger of the situation. Elliot and his friends could do whatever they wished now that they were completely away from the bustle of traffic. Clipper thought about backing away, but as his right hand shifted the car into reverse, Elliot opened his door and pulled out a shotgun.

"Stop!" Elliot demanded. "You know, you are really an annoyance."

Clipper swallowed, speechless and terrified.

"Get off our tail. You understand?"

"There's no way you"ll come clean from this. I had someone call the police," Clipper warned as his heart raced.

"Bring em on. The more the merrier," Elliot said as he trotted over to Clipper's car and aimed the gun at his right front tire. BAM. Clipper flinched at the sound of live ammo and the pop of his tire. Although he winced, he felt a strange sense of relief that Elliot aimed at rubber and not at his head. Elliot took a few steps and then aimed his gun at the other tire. Cha-ching.

"Don't even think of ruining your rims on some stupid chase," Elliot said with a devilish smile. Finally, he ran back to his car and tossed the gun to one of his friends. Clipper only caught a glimpse of A. C.'s face. A. C. looked like a zombie, as if he had already been murdered. No expression. No movement. Not even a glance in Clipper's direction.

A voice from inside the car yelled to Elliot, "They're here! Get in and let's go!"

Elliot shifted to drive and jumped a median with the Camaro as he made a quick U-turn. Clipper's eyes darted to the end of the road and saw three police cars closing in on the scene. Two of the cars turned around as Elliot raced passed them—half on the road and half on the median. They continued the pursuit and the other patrol car raced to where Clipper stood. An officer rolled down the window and yelled, "You all right? Who's with you?"

"Nobody," Clipper replied.

"Hop in," the officer ordered.

Clipper got in and they drove off, abandoning Clipper's crippled car.

They hung back, following the chase cautiously with the aid of the police radio.

"You are lucky they didn't stick a bullet in you, kid. Don't ever try that again," the officer said.

Clipper nodded. "I panicked. A. C.'s a good friend of mine."

"Then you should be careful who you hang around with," the officer said. After a few moments of listening to the police radio the officer looked over at Clipper. "But I can't say that I wouldn't have done the same thing," he said half smiling.

In a matter of minutes the ordeal ended as four police cars eliminated every option available to Elliot. He slammed on his brakes and tried to look as innocent as one could possibly look with a swarm of law enforcement officers surrounding the Camaro with guns drawn. The police ordered them all to get out and lie face down on the ground.

Clipper looked on in amazement as the police searched the car. They found four automatic weapons under the seat and enough ammunition to fortify a small army in the tool case located in the trunk. Within five minutes, TV crews and reporters descended on the scene.

"Everything's going to be OK," Clipper said to A. C., who looked over with eyes that seemed very distant. Clipper knew his friend didn't want to talk. "I'll call you," he said. A. C. just nodded.

Clipper returned to his car and opened the door when A. C. yelled, "Thanks, Clipper."

"No need to thank me. I was just an observer," Clipper called back with a smile. As he turned the ignition Clipper whispered a prayer: "Forgive me, Father, for not trusting You."

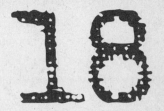

That evening Kandi, Justin, Autumn, and Clipper went out to eat at their old place of employment, the BurgeRama. "Sure feels good to be on this side of the counter," Justin said as he sat down at the table.

"Got that right," Clipper said.

"So tell me," Autumn asked Clipper, "Do you think A. C.'s on the verge of a turnaround?"

"I don't know. I thought I'd give him some time before I start the samurai evangelism technique," Clipper said smiling. "I hope things settle down. I'm tired of all the craziness. Guys planting bombs, threatening churches, friends on drugs, people stealing computers, politicians making passes at high school students. What ever happened to Mayberry? Where's Barney Fife? If he were here, he'd nip it. Nip it in the bud!" Clipper said in his best Don Knotts voice.

"I just have a feeling things are going to return to normal," Kandi said.

"I don't know if I want normal," Clipper shot back. "Normal is weird these days. I want boring, which used to be normal until weird became normal."

The others laughed.

"I'm serious," Clipper said.

A beeper interrupted their conversation. All four students drew their beepers in front of them like swords.

"Not mine."

"Me neither."

"I got it," Kandi said.

"Who is it?" Justin asked, looking over Kandi's shoulder at the number.

"I don't know. I'll be right back," Kandi walked out of the BurgeRama to the side of the building where the pay phone was. She dialed the number and waited for an answer.

After one ring someone picked up. "Hello."

Kandi recognized the voice. "Jill?"

"Hey, Kandi," Jill said. There was silence and then Kandi heard Jill's voice crack. She said through her tears, "Zack left and nobody can find him. He called me, and he sounded crazy. He said he wanted to thank me. He wanted to say goodbye. He screamed at me and told me to forget about him."

"OK, Jill. You stay there in case he calls back. Does he have a cell phone?" Kandi asked.

"In his car. But I've tried that. He's not answering," Jill replied frantically. "You need to pick me up! I need to find him!" she said louder.

"Jill, we'll look but I think—"

"Pick me up!" Jill exclaimed.

"All right. Justin and I will be there in a minute."

"Thanks."

Kandi walked back into the BurgeRama. "Justin, we've got to go. Zack's acting crazy. He's gone off, and no one knows where he went."

"Wait a sec. We'll come too," Clipper said as he and Autumn automatically rose to their feet as well.

"Why don't you two try the school. Kandi and I will drive around and see if we can spot his Jeep. You've got my beeper number. Page me if you find him," Justin said as he and Kandi scurried out of the restaurant, leaving their half-eaten supper on the table.

"See what I mean by normal being weird and weird being normal?" Clipper said to Autumn.

Justin and Kandi picked up Jill and then went to the school, which happened to be open for rehearsals and athletics. Zack was nowhere to be found. Jill was completely distraught as the three of them tried to figure out where Zack could be.

"I think I know where he might be," Kandi said suddenly.

"Where?" Justin asked.

"The quarry," she replied.

"I don't think I remember how to get there," Justin said.

"Let's just head in that direction. I think I can remember the turnoff," Kandi said.

They were all quiet as Justin drove, using every mental resource and memory they had to recall the gravel road that led to the site.

"Hey!" Kandi said.

"Hey what?"

"I remember there was a billboard for some bar right before the road," Kandi said.

"Kandi's photographic memory comes through. I just hope the negatives aren't distorted in the dark room," Justin said without smiling.

"How can you joke at a time like this?" Kandi said looking over at him.

"Got to deal with the stress somehow," he replied.

Jill sat in the back seat hugging her knees to her chest and crying softly. Five minutes later, they found the road. The cloud of dust that enveloped them as they drove down the road indicated someone must have beaten them to the quarry just moments before.

Just ahead they saw Eli's car and Zack's Jeep. Clipper trotted over to them as Justin parked.

"Eli's here too?" Kandi said.

"We went by to pick him up and he offered to drive," Clipper said breathlessly. "He knew where the place was. He's gone down there to check on Zack." They looked down from the steep overhang, and they could dimly see Zack's very still body on the bank of the quarry.

"No! No!" Jill cried out hysterically. "He's dead!"

"We don't know that!" Autumn said, trying to hold on to the distraught girl.

Without a word Justin and Clipper joined Eli on a thorny descent down to the base of the man-made cliff. "We're coming, Zack."

Autumn raced back to Eli's car, reached into the glove compartment and found a flashlight. "God, please let it work," she whispered as she flipped it on. "Yes!"

She ran back to the edge and tried to light Eli's way as he approached Zack. The beam was no match for the darkness surrounding them. After some difficulty, Eli finally reached bottom and ran to Zack's side.

"He's unconscious, but he has a pulse, a really fast one. We've got to get him up there and to the hospital!" Eli screamed.

"I'll call 9-1-1," Autumn replied.

"We don't have time for that. We're bringing him up," Eli replied, sounding panicked by the task before him.

"You're wrong, Eli. We can't do that. He may have broken his back or something. Call 9-1-1 and tell them you'll meet them at the gas station back on the Highway 301," Justin said frantically.

As Autumn ran back to Eli's car, Eli looked at Justin and said, "I hope you're right."

"We can't afford to be wrong. He could have fallen. I don't want to take the chance of causing any paralysis. We could lose him halfway up the climb," Justin said.

"You're right," Eli agreed.

For twenty minutes they waited. Clipper, Justin, and Eli huddled around him wondering if he would make it. They covered him with Eli's jacket and tried to keep him warm.

Out of nowhere Justin said quietly, "Lord, don't let him slip away. Give him another chance. We don't know what's going on, but don't let him die out here."

In a matter of seconds after the prayer, the flashing ambulance lights cut through the moonless sky.

Detective Fuller separated Elliot from the other two young men, pulling him into an office at the police station.

"You don't have any proof. I didn't have anything to do with this," Elliot shouted.

"Then why were you taking A. C. by force after we released him?" Fuller asked angrily.

"Cuz he lied about us. How could you be so stupid? He's really pulled the wool over your eyes. It was his idea. He made the bomb. His fingerprints were all over that place."

"How do you know that?"

"He told me," Elliot replied.

"He did?"

"Sure he did," Elliot said confidently. "There's no way you found anything on any of us."

"So you kept the place pretty clean. You used gloves." Fuller said.

"Aren't you listening? I didn't do it!" Elliot yelled.

"I have someone who said they saw a car like yours at the church a few minutes before the alarm sounded."

"That's impossible. Your eyewitness is A. C." Elliot said confidently. "Can't you see that he's lying to save his own skin?"

"Wrong again, Elliot. The witness is the lady who lives across from the church. You thought you were so clean." Fuller sat down behind his cluttered desk and laughed quietly, shaking his head. "Only problem is you didn't count on A. C. getting involved."

"So what? Some old lady saw a car like mine. You still don't have a case," Elliot proclaimed with a smile.

"Oh, yeah. Listen to this," Fuller said as he reached over to a shelf for a small cassette player and pressed play.

A.C.: So what? It's over. They've got me here and you're free. You should be celebrating.

Elliot: You think you're safe in there? You're not. Understand? I'll kill you for turning on us. I swear I will. It wasn't enough for you just to drop out of the plan, but you had to stop it. You'll regret it.

A.C.: I don't care anymore.

Elliot: I promise you'll never stop our plans. The wrath of The Association is something you can't comprehend.

Elliot let out an animalistic roar as he dove for the tape player. Two guards rushed in to restrain him.

"I thought you were smarter than that. Just totally slipped your mind that we might be monitoring his calls," Fuller said matter-of-factly as he stood to leave. "Send him and his pals to maximum security and keep them separated, even if that means shipping the other two to Shelbyville."

Autumn, Jill, and Justin remained in the ICU waiting room that night, along with Zack's parents. Mr. and Mrs. Galloway were in total shock, silent mostly, with only an occasional soft whisper to each other. Their devastation couldn't be masked.

Finally Mr. Galloway walked across the waiting room and gestured for Justin to follow. They walked down to an empty hospital room, and Mr. Galloway closed the door. Justin's anxiety grew as Zack's dad paused for a moment.

"I'm trying to understand how all this happened," Mr. Galloway began. "Who did this to my son?"

"I'm sorry, sir, I don't know," Justin replied. "We thought something must be going on, and when we asked him about it, he just laughed it off or lied about it."

"Well, I want to find out how this all started. Who was he hanging around with? What about this girl—Kandi? What about Jill?" Mr. Galloway asked.

"I don't really know Jill. But I do know Kandi. She's not involved in any groups that use drugs," Justin said.

"He's such a good kid. We've never doubted his integrity. He's so smart and talented. And he has a great sense of humor. I thought he had it all," Mr. Galloway said.

"I know."

"And now he could die."

Justin just nodded, wishing he knew the right thing to say.

An hour passed with no word from the medical staff. Clipper walked into the waiting room with some food his parents had prepared. "Any word?" he whispered to Justin.

"No," Justin said quietly.

"Where are Zack's parents?" Clipper asked.

"The nurse said that they could go back there to see him. But he's still unconscious," Kandi replied.

"They're in total shock. They didn't have a clue," Justin added and then took a bite of one of the sandwiches. "Thanks for the food," he said.

"You know moms," Clipper said smiling. "The world could be falling apart, and they just want to make sure no one has to face it on an empty stomach."

Justin and the others smiled.

"Eli took Autumn home," Justin said.

Clipper surveyed Justin's ragged appearance. They both had nicks and cuts from the trek down into the quarry. Clipper's scrapes had been cleaned up by his mom when he went home, but Justin still had on the tattered clothes from the rescue. "You look like garbage," Clipper said.

"Thanks, buddy," Justin replied.

All eyes turned to the outside door as it opened. Clipper was shocked when he saw A. C. He walked over and shook his hand.

"I called your house," A. C. said. "Your mom said you'd be here. How's the guy doing?" he asked, awkwardly.

"We don't know. Haven't heard a word," Clipper said quietly.

"Just thought I'd drop by and check on him," A. C. said.

Kandi spoke up. "Hey, A. C., we've got some food here. You hungry?"

"I'm starving," A. C. said.

Clipper couldn't believe it. *A.C. actually expressed a need!* Clipper thought to himself. *Small miracle, but I'll take it.* "We were about to pray," Clipper said to A. C.

Kandi threw him a confused glance as if to say, "We were?"

"Right," Justin said.

"Want to join us?" Clipper said to A. C.

"Uh . . . no thanks," A. C. said with a touch of embarrassment.

As they prayed, A. C. leaned against the wall a few feet from them with his arms crossed.

As the others took turns praying, Clipper wondered what A. C. thought about the whole deal. He dared not peek. He didn't want A. C. to suspect that he had initiated the prayer partly on A. C.'s behalf, even though he did. Clipper just hoped that A. C. would still be around after they finished. Amazingly, A. C. stayed right there next to them; his face seemed tense, as if his mind was a battlefield.

It was two o'clock, long after the students had left, when a doctor shared the news with Zack's parents—their son's condition had stabilized. He had miraculously made it out of the woods.

At the Grace Home for Girls, Jenny was awakened at the same time by one of the home parents.

"Jenny?" she said. "I'm sorry to disturb you. Your father's here. He said that he needed to see you. He said it was an emergency."

The voice from outside her door frightened her. She felt sure something terrible had happened. She turned on the lamp on her nightstand and sat up slowly in bed.

"I'm coming," she said sleepily.

"Actually, he's right here," the attendant said as she stepped out of the room.

"Jenny, please. I need to talk to you," her father said, his voice edged with anxiety.

Jenny got out of her bed and opened the door. She saw her dad, who was soaked from the brief dash from his car into the building in the sudden torrent of a late night storm. She had never seen him in such pitiful shape. He seemed distraught, almost childlike.

"What's going on? Is Mom OK?" she asked.

"She's fine. I haven't been able to sleep for the past few nights. I keep seeing you slipping away from me. I've been so concerned about my perfect world. I've always been a perfectionist. I couldn't believe that I—"

"Daddy, I'm the one who started this whole mess," Jenny said.

"But, honey, I never thought that I'd ever stoop so low as when I asked you to cover up this pregnancy. I know that I didn't support you. I haven't supported you at all. I've replayed the moment you told us over and over and I can't live with myself. I . . . I actually hoped you'd fix the problem with an abortion," her father sobbed.

"The thing that I think about when I go to bed and the moment that I wake up is that I've tried to save my own reputation, my own face. That's not what being a dad is supposed to be about." Mr. Elton's face contorted in pain as he cried. "I should have cared about you and made sure you knew I loved you no matter what. I should have supported you."

Jenny began to weep. She'd never seen this man who raised her, who tutored her, who at one time guarded her future, become so utterly broken.

"I've done it all wrong the past few months. I'm sorry, Jenny. I'm so very sorry. I know I'll never be able to regain those months with you. I've lost them forever. I just want you to come home."

Could this be a dream? Jenny wondered, as he sat there next to her on the bed. "What about Mom?" she asked.

"Your mom feels the same way I do. I think she was just waiting for me to come to my senses. She's always trusted me. Maybe she trusted me too much," her dad speculated. "Get some rest, and I'll be back in the morning to pick you up," he said as he stood.

"I love you, Daddy," Jenny cried, throwing her arms around her father's neck.

"I love you too."

A. C. caught the morning news. He had been cleared of any wrongdoing. Detective Fuller had turned out to be a nice guy after all. He told the press that A. C. had aided them in capturing the culprits. It was true, but they could have said lots more. He returned to school that day, where they canceled the recommended expulsion. Lots of students tried to talk to him, but he rarely did more than nod and move away.

After school he went to the police station and walked in to Detective Fuller's office.

"I'm surprised to see you, kid. I thought you'd want to stay as far away from me as possible."

A. C. smiled. "You're not so bad," he said.

"Darn right, I'm not. You owe me big time," Fuller replied.

"I wanted to ask a favor of you," A. C. said.

"Ask away. I'll just add it to the tab."

"I want to see Elliot," A. C. replied.

After a pause, Fuller exhaled in disbelief, "You're kidding, right?"

"You know I don't kid around like that. I want to talk to him," A. C. replied firmly.

"Why?" Fuller asked, puzzled.

"I just need to close the book on the whole deal. I have something I need to tell him," A. C. explained.

"You know the way things work up there. It's not the most private place for exchanging secrets," Fuller said.

"Don't have any secrets, Fuller. Wire me if you want. Like I said, I just need to see him," A. C. said.

Knowing the stubbornness of who he was dealing with, Fuller finally relented.

An hour later A. C. entered the visitation room at the county jail and waited for the string of obscenities Elliot would use to greet him. He wasn't disappointed. When Elliot saw his visitor, expletives spewed forth volcanically. He spit at the glass that separated the two of them.

Elliot finally settled down and then hissed, "I don't ever want to see you alive again. You are as good as dead. I will get out of here, and I will find you."

A. C. said nothing.

"How can you live with yourself, traitor? You're as guilty as I am. You just happened to be a snitch," Elliot said.

To A. C., Elliot looked like an rabid animal, entrapped, wounded, and ready to pounce if he could. Bruises covered his face from several attempts to resist the police and jailers during the booking process.

"Why did you even come here? They sent you here, didn't they? They want more information."

A. C. shook his head. "No. I asked to see you."

"Why?" Elliot said.

"I can't really say why. I just wanted to look you in the eye and tell you that I'm not afraid of you anymore."

"You should be," Elliot replied. He turned and banged on the door for the jailer to remove him from the visitation booth, still threatening and cursing A. C. as he exited.

A. C. walked out of the building feeling good about himself. When he came to see Elliot, he really didn't have an answer to the question of why he needed to do it. But as he left, he understood. He needed to see one last time where he had been just a few weeks before. In Elliot's eyes he saw the kind of person he used to be and potentially could still be if he chose to walk down that path again. He realized what his life could have been. He wondered what made the difference. Why did he lay down that lifestyle? It was so seductive and pleasurable, but now he knew that its end was total destruction.

He pulled into the traffic without a clue of where he wanted to go. He just wanted to drive and think. He looked at the CDs s next to him. Korn, Marilyn Manson, Nirvana, Metallica . . . In the past, slipping a CD into the dash was simply a part of starting the car, but he didn't this time. He drove in total silence.

After a few minutes he was on an open road. He suddenly felt weak and unsteady, so he pulled over to the side. He opened the door and got out, looking at the trees and feeling the cool breeze. The sun was setting. He wondered if he had ever stopped to see a sunset in his life. He felt free. He felt alone, but not the kind of loneliness that plagued him for years. This loneliness came from a desire to be new.

"God," he whispered. "I don't know what to say. I don't think I've ever really talked to You like this. I'm not a praying guy. Never have been. But if You're out there, I just want You to show me who You are. I always thought You were the enemy—the One who enjoyed messing my life up and condemning me for all my mistakes. I don't think that anymore. I want to learn who You are. I want You to be part of my life."

For the first time in his life, he felt acceptance. It seemed strange, wonderful, and new.

Kandi didn't know what to say when Zack showed up at her door that Friday afternoon.

"Hey, Kandi," Zack said, a timid smile on his face.

Kandi had never seen him like that. "It's great to see you. Pretty miraculous, actually," she said awkwardly.

"I know," Zack said.

"What happens now?" she asked him.

"I guess it's time to rebuild," Zack said.

"The rough part's over," said Kandi.

"I wouldn't go that far. I'm going into a treatment center tonight. So I'm enjoying my last few moments of precious freedom."

"I'm proud of you," Kandi said.

"How can you say that?" Zack said emotionally.

Kandi didn't know how to respond to his question. "I just know where you've been and where you are now. I just feel proud for you."

"I'm pretty ashamed," Zack said as he wiped a tear from his face. "I'm scared. I don't know if I can do this. There's not much left of me. I'm pretty spent. I've been putting on quite a show for the past few months, and I'm really tired."

Kandi embraced him. She had never seen a guy that was as broken as Zack seemed to be.

"I don't think I have the courage to be me. I don't know who I am anymore," he said, sobbing into her shoulder.

"We'll pray for you," Kandi replied as they broke from the embrace.

"Thanks. I really mean that. I never really thought much about God until everything fell apart," Zack said.

"Crisis has a way of doing that," Kandi said with a quiet laugh.

"I want to apologize for blowing you off when you and Autumn tried to talk to me. I was just running scared. I know I almost destroyed your relationship with Justin on top of everything else."

"Don't think about that. You just get better, and we'll see you when you get back."

As he walked away, she felt an overwhelming appreciation for Justin and all the stability he gave her when her life seemed so out of balance.

"I don't think I've ever met a girl like you before," he said, turning back around.

"I'd have to say that my feeling for you is definitely mutual," Kandi said with a knowing smile.

Clipper didn't mind that Coach Tupper had planned an early Saturday morning basketball practice that lasted well into the afternoon. He had spent so much time analyzing, soul searching, rediscovering, and bargaining with God that he welcomed the grueling physical workout. The previous year basketball had been his obsession. He thought about how much things had changed since then.

As he walked away out of the locker room and back onto the court after a quick shower, he stopped dead in his tracks. *That can't be Jenny,* he thought to himself when he looked across the gym at the lone girl sitting in the bleachers. She stood up and walked slowly over to him. Her presence calmed his spirit.

"You're back," he said, a slow smile lighting up his face.

"I wanted to surprise you," Jenny said as she made her way to him, reaching out for his hand.

He embraced her gently and began to weep.

"Are you OK?" she whispered.

"Never better," he replied. "Just seeing you here. That's all I wanted, really. Just to see you here."

"I was worried. I've been afraid that you'd look at me differently if I came back. It's one thing to care for some girl who's seven months pregnant in another state. But to have to put up with her on a day-to-day basis?" Jenny said, half joking.

"I have no idea what that means," Clipper said, stroking her hair. "Are your mom and dad OK?"

"They're healing, just like I'm healing," Jenny said. "I think you bothered them so much with common sense that they finally surrendered to reality. Who knows? They might end up forgiving me after all."

"Of course they will," Clipper said.

"They aren't bad parents. They just have lots of pain right now. I can't say that I blame them."

"So how did you get here?" Clipper asked. "You didn't drive here all by yourself, did you?"

"Kandi picked me up," Jenny replied.

Clipper laughed, "As usual, I'm always the last to find out."

Thanks for visiting Summit High. I'd love to hear from you
if you ever want to ask a question, swap stories,
need prayer, or even vent about life in general.
My E-mail address is mtullos@lifeway.com
See ya!
Matt Tullos